"Drink this," he said. It was a command

"What is it?" Jilly asked warily, her senses still reeling from her brush with drowning.

"Cognac," Edouard said.

"I don't want it. What are you trying to do? Make me drunk?"

"Oh, sure, so I can take advantage of you during the night," he scoffed. "What has happened to you in your short life to make you so suspicious of a guy? Did your late lamented do this to you?"

"Of course not! Kevin was kind and gentle. It's just that you—" She broke off, not wanting him to know the effect he had on her.

His glance flashed to her face, and suddenly he stroked a finger down her pale cheek. Hazily she thought, he shouldn't be touching her. That was breaking the ground rules she'd laid down.

His hand continued its caress. She was suddenly filled with an aching need to forget her ground rules....

FLORA KIDD had a romantic dream—to own a sailboat and learn how to sail it. That dream came true when she found romance of another sort with a man who shared her love of the sea and became her husband and father of their four children. A native of Scotland, this bestselling romance author now lives in New Brunswick, one of Canada's maritime provinces, with the sea on her doorstep.

Books by Flora Kidd

HARLEQUIN PRESENTS
682—PASSIONATE PURSUIT
729—DESPERATE DESIRE
756—THE OPEN MARRIAGE
771—FLIGHT TO PASSION
834—A SECRET PLEASURE
848—THE ARROGANT LOVER
970—PASSIONATE CHOICE
995—THE MARRIED LOVERS
1024—MASQUERADE MARRIAGE
1058—BELOVED DECEIVER

HARLEQUIN ROMANCE
2146—TO PLAY WITH FIRE
2228—THE BARGAIN BRIDE

Don't miss any of our special offers. Write to us at the following address for information on our newest releases.

Harlequin Reader Service
901 Fuhrmann Blvd., P.O. Box 1397, Buffalo, NY 14240
Canadian address: P.O. Box 603,
Fort Erie, Ont. L2A 5X3

FLORA KIDD

when lovers meet

Harlequin Books

TORONTO • NEW YORK • LONDON
AMSTERDAM • PARIS • SYDNEY • HAMBURG
STOCKHOLM • ATHENS • TOKYO • MILAN

Harlequin Presents first edition July 1988
ISBN 0-373-11091-X

Original hardcover edition published in 1987
by Mills & Boon Limited

CHAPTER ONE

IT was close to sunset time, almost six o'clock on St Mark's, a mountainous island in the West Indies, half under French rule and half under Dutch rule, with many beaches of golden sand that attract hundreds of tourists each winter. Feathery cirrus clouds, stained crimson and gold, streaked the sky, and shadows from exotic shrubs and trees were long and purple across the driveway that curved round to a house on the French side of the island, known as La Maison des Colombiers, the House of Doves.

Jilly Carter turned the small Korean car, provided for her use by the company for which she worked, into the parking-space beneath the down-dipping branches of some poinciana trees. She put on the brake and turned off the engine. She had lived in the house for almost a month and she still felt a wonderful feeling of satisfaction whenever she returned to it each evening. She would live in it for another three months, February, March and April, looking after it for its owner, who was away in France making a film.

Michelle Martin, the owner of the house, was a French film actress who had been born on the island and who could easily have rented out the house for those three months to winter tourists, thought Jilly, as she collected up the groceries she had bought before leaving the car. But because the actress had had a bad experience with tenants the previous year she had decided this time, when she had been called away to France, to have someone she knew and trusted to live in it. At the time Jilly had been looking for accommodation and had been recommended to Michelle by Irma Stratton, a New Yorker who ran a real-estate business on the island, renting out houses and apartments as well as advertising property for sale.

Opening the door of the car ready to get out, Jilly paused, her eyes opening wide. Another car was in the parking-space, parked a little nearer the house. It was dark grey and was difficult to see in the shadows, but she might not have noticed it if the chrome of its bumpers hadn't glinted in the last of rays of light slanting up from the sun which had sunk below the horizon.

Clutching the bag of groceries, she got out of the car, slammed the door shut and after another puzzled glance at the shadowy grey car, headed for the house, following a path that twisted between oleander and hibiscus bushes. Reaching the wide terrace in front of the house, she stopped in her tracks. The floodlights were on, illuminating the kidney-shaped swimming-pool and the apron of reddish-brown tiles surrounding it. Her glance swerved to the house. The double glass-panelled front doors were wide open and light from inside lamps streamed out of the opening.

Hesitating no longer, she bounded up the shallow steps that led to the entrance of the house, her mind flicking over the possibility that Michelle had returned unexpectedly. Yet that wasn't the actress's car parked in the parking-space. Michelle owned a Citroën. The car in the space was definitely American and the Citroën was in a service garage on the Dutch side of the island, where it would stay until Michelle returned.

In the kitchen, which was located in the middle of the sprawling ranch-style house, she put down the bag of groceries and stood still, listening. From the direction of the west wing came the sound of rushing water. Someone must be in the bathroom showering. The question was—*who*? Her lips tightening, Jilly looked around for a suitable weapon and found none. Pulling open a drawer she searched for and found a carving-knife. The wicked-looking blade shimmered on the light shed from the fluorescent tube overhead. With the wooden handle clutched in her hand and the blade pointing forwards, Jilly made for the passage that led to the suite of rooms in the west wing. Lights blazed overhead and from every doorway. Whoever was in the house didn't seem to care about being discovered and she probably didn't need the weapon. Still, it was best to be sure when she was responsible for looking after the house. Someone had entered without her permission and had to be confronted.

When she reached the door of the west-wing bathroom she stood outside hesitating again. Through the door came, not the sound of rushing water, but a pleasant baritone voice singing a popular song. Jilly thumped on the door with a clenched fist and, with the knife pointed towards the door, she waited for a response. The voice broke off in the middle of a word. There was silence. Jilly thumped on the door again and shouted,

'Open this door. I want to know who you are.'

Another brief silence, then the door was swung slowly back. A tall, wide-shouldered man stood in the opening. His hairy, sun-tanned chest was naked and a bath towel was draped around his hips. Wet fringes of dark hair hung over his forehead, and from beneath level eyebrows his vivid blue eyes regarded her narrowly.

'Who are you?' he challenged her. His sharp-angled jaw was blurred by black beard stubble and his teeth flashed white against the darkness of his face. When he saw the knife pointing at him his eyes widened in surprise and he stepped back a pace, watching the knife warily.

'Tell me who you are first and what you're doing in this house,' insisted Jilly, the hand holding the knife dropping to her side. In his unshaven condition with muscles bulging and rippling beneath his tawny skin he looked more than tough but something in the direct glance of his clear eyes and the proud carriage of his head convinced her that he wasn't criminal in any way.

'Would you believe I'm a relative of Michelle's?' he replied coolly. 'Her elder brother, in fact.'

'You're not French,' Jilly accused. He spoke English without much of an accent. A slight smile lifted one corner of his mouth as he acknowledged the truth of her accusation.

'Not entirely,' he agreed. 'But then neither is Michelle. Our father was English.' He frowned suddenly and impatiently. 'But why the hell should I tell you anything about myself? You're the stranger here. Not me. What right have you to question me?'

'I have every right. I'm living in this house and looking after it for the next three months while Mademoiselle Martin is in France making a film,' Jilly asserted.

'Oh, yeah?' he jeered sceptically. 'When I last talked to Michelle she said nothing about your coming with house.' His glance swept over her insolently and his wide lips took on a mocking curve. 'I suppose she guessed I'd be in need of more than food and a place to lay my head when I got here,' he added suggestively. 'And she chose well. I'm rather partial to blondes.'

'Are you telling me that Michelle said you can stay in this house?' demanded Jilly sharply, ignoring his insolence. 'When did she tell you that?'

'I guess it must have been last spring some time before I went to Europe. We agreed that I should come to live in the house when I got here.' Water dripped from his hair down his face and he wiped it away with the back of his hand. 'Look, I'd like to get dry and into some clothes so that we can continue this conversation in a more comfortable situation. And without the carving knife.' A slight grin curved his lips. 'While you're threatening to stab me and I'm in a state of near nudity I feel at a distinct disadvantage.'

Jilly looked down at the knife in her hand as if she was surprised to find she was still holding it, then shook her head from side to side so that her straight shining hair shimmered silkily.

'You have to admit that I have reason to be threatening, coming back here and finding the house wide open, light streaming out of it and a strange car parked in the parking-space,' she argued. 'I thought someone must have broken in and I'm still not sure whether I should believe your story. No one has said anything to me about Michelle's brother coming to stay here.'

'Michelle said nothing to me about having let the house to a belligerent little Brit, either,' he retorted. 'The phone is ringing,' he added laconically and stepping back into the bathroom shut the door.

He was right, the phone-bell was shrilling. Jilly rushed back to the kitchen still armed with the carving knife.

Picking up the receiver she spoke breathlessly into the mouthpiece.

'Hello. Jilly Carter speaking.'

'Jilly. So glad to get you at last.' There was no mistaking Irma Stratton's nasal twang.

'Irma, listen,' Jilly broke in impetuously. 'There's a man in the house. He says he's Michelle's brother and . . .'

'He's got there already?' Irma's voice went up a couple of tones higher. 'I was hoping to warn you about him before he arrived, and I guess I would have done if only you'd been in the house when I first phoned.'

'I had to stop to get groceries and there was a big line up at the check-out counter. Is he really Michelle's brother?'

'It's true. Isn't he something? He walked into my office this afternoon and demanded a key to the house.'

'But how can you be sure he's Michelle's brother?' exclaimed Jilly. 'He doesn't look much like her. Didn't you ask for some form of identification before giving him a key?'

'I can be sure because I've met him before, two years ago when he was here on the island,' said Irma, with a touch of dryness. 'And you have to agree that once met he's not easily forgotten.'

'You'll want me to move out then,' said Jilly, hiding her disappointment as she always did by speaking abruptly.

'No, no. The arrangement I made was with Michelle for you to stay until she returns. He won't be there long. Maybe a couple of weeks. He never stays long anywhere. OK?'

'I suppose so,' muttered Jilly.

'If you have any problems with him just give me a call. I have to go now. We're having people to dinner and this place is just a mess. Must clear up. See you, Jilly.'

'See you . . . oh, wait, just one more thing . . .' Jilly broke off. Irma had already hung up. No chance to ask her what Michelle's brother was called.

Slowly she laid the receiver on its rest. She was still holding the carving-knife. Her lips twisting wryly as she realised how foolish she must have seemed to the man in the bathroom when she had brandished the knife at him, she opened the drawer and put it away, turning quickly to the doorway that led to the west wing when she heard footsteps.

Freshly shaved, wearing much-faded jeans and a thin white shirt, he seemed bigger and more muscular than ever. His black hair was waving and curling about his ears as it dried and, against the teak-coloured tan of his face, his eyes looked very blue. He paused just inside the kitchen and stared at her warily. Jilly decided to take the initiative.

'Hi,' she said, holding out her right hand. 'I'm Jilly Carter. Irma Stratton was just on the phone. She explained about you. I'd have known about you before you arrived if I'd got here a little sooner than I did. Sorry I was so belligerent.'

His dark eyebrows tilted and his smile flashed giving his face a wicked yet breathtaking charm. Jilly caught her breath and felt her knees wobble. Never in the whole of her life had she reacted like that to a man's smile. His big hand grasped hers. She could feel hard calluses on his fingers and palms and guessed he had been sailing recently.

'I'm Ed Forster, Michelle's black sheep of a brother, always turning up when I'm least expected. And in case you're wondering why my last name is different from hers it's because she uses our mother's family name for professional purposes. Something to do with Michelle Martin being more alliterative and therefore more memorable,' he said with a touch of mockery. 'Did Irma vouch for me?'

'Yes, she did. Ed short for Edward?' she asked lightly, pulling her hand free of his grasp. He had a grip that seemed to possess and then demand.

'Ed short for Edouard. My mother insisted on the French spelling.' There was a short silence as they eyed each other cautiously. Then, 'How long have you been on the island?' he asked casually.

'Nearly seven months.'

'That's some vacation you're having,' he remarked, watching her closely, almost suspiciously. 'Are you here legally?'

'I'm not on vacation and I am here legally,' she replied coolly. She was accustomed by now to having her legal status questioned. 'I work at Seasails, the sail-making business run by Piet Block at the boatyard in Williamsburg.'

'The authorities allow you to work on the island?' he queried on a note of surprise. 'I thought only natives of the island could work here.'

'That is the rule, yes, but when it is a job for which no islander is qualified a company is allowed to employ a foreigner. When he found out I'm a trained sailmaker Piet offered me the job of being the chief designer and supervisor of the new sail-loft he was setting up. He arranged with the authorities for my work permit,' she replied, then swung away to unpack the grocery bag. She was finding his presence rather overwhelming, something to do with the masculine vitality that seemed to radiate from him plus the mesmerising stare of his intensely blue eyes.

Behind her she heard the fridge door open and shut. It

was followed by the snap of metal as he opened the can of beer he had taken out. Escaping air hissed. She began to unpack the grocery bag.

'That doesn't explain how you happened to be on the island when Piet offered you the job,' he drawled. 'How come you were washed up on this particular island? Like all the rest of the Brits, Aussies, and South Africans who live here? Did you come on a yacht?'

'Yes, I did.' She turned to look at him again. He was leaning against one of the counters, beer-can in hand.

'Across the Atlantic? But not alone, surely?' His glance swept her from head to foot again and dismissed the idea that she was capable of managing a yacht on her own.

'No, not alone. I was a member of a crew on a sixty-foot ketch belonging to Reg Turner. He was, at the time, commodore of the cruising club where I lived in England. We—that is, the sailmaking company I worked for there—made the sails for the ketch. Reg invited me to be a member of the crew when he decided to cruise to the Caribbean and then up to the States and Canada.'

'Were you the only woman on board?' he asked casually, seemingly more interested in the can of beer than her, but she guessed what lay behind his question. He wanted to know if she had been Reg's sleeping companion.

'No, I wasn't. Reg's wife and daughter were on board too,' she replied and turned back to the groceries. She wasn't going to tell him any more about herself, why she had jumped at Reg's invitation to leave England and sail away to the tropics. 'I'm having chicken for dinner tonight,' she went on rather reluctantly. 'You're welcome to have some.'

'Does this show of hospitality mean you're going to stay

in the house?' he asked.

'Irma said you'll only be here a couple of weeks and that Michelle would prefer it if I did stay,' she replied diffidently. 'Do you mind if I stay on? It's awfully hard to find accommodation on the island right now. Until Irma arranged with Michelle for me to stay here I had to live aboard a boat belonging to Gerry and Sue Leigh. There wasn't much privacy.'

'No, I don't mind. I noticed you'd chosen a room in the east wing so I moved into the west wing. We shan't get in each other's way too much. Probably we'll see more of each other at the boatyard than here. I'm having my boat hauled out there and hope to be working on it.'

'Where have you come from?' she asked, opening the fridge door and pushing packages of frozen food into the freezer compartment.

'Just now I've come from Miami. I sailed there from Newport, Rhode Island last November. Which part of England do you come from? I was in Plymouth before I left to sail across the ocean to Newport last June.'

'The south coast. From a little village near Portsmouth. You won't have heard of it, I expect. It's called Felton,' she said distantly and began to busy herself searching cupboards, opening and closing doors, in an attempt to hint to him that she had no wish to continue the conversation.

'Do you always slam cupboard doors when you're mad about something?' The pleasantly drawling voice held a note of amusement and she swung round again to find he was standing close to her. He advanced a step, the glance of his blue eyes lingering provocatively on her hair, her eyes, her lips. '*La fille aux cheveux de lin*,' he murmured, adding when she looked puzzled, 'The Girl with the Flaxen Hair.

It's the title of a piano piece by Debussy. He could have had someone like you in mind when he composed it. Is your hair naturally flaxen or is it dyed?'

Jilly made a great effort to control a sudden turmoil of emotion. The time had come, she decided, to lay down some ground rules if she was going to share this house with him.

'It's natural,' she said tersely. 'And I think I'd better make something quite clear before we go any further, a rule I hope you'll keep. It's to be strictly hands off. I'm not available. Just because I'm going to be living in this house while you're staying here doesn't mean I'm willing to sleep with you.'

'Now whatever put it into your head that I might want to sleep with you?' he taunted. 'You seem much too young and too inexperienced for a guy like me and . . .'

'I'll have you know I'm twenty-five, nearly twenty-six, and I've been married,' she interrupted him angrily, falling into the trap he had set for her.

'Really?' Tilted black eyebrows mocked her while blue eyes sparkled with amusement. 'I would never have believed it. Such fine smooth skin, such clear eyes, such an air of innocence. So you've been married. And divorced, perhaps?'

'No. Kevin died. In an accident. He was driving too fast, as usual,' she said tonelessly. She'd managed it. For the first time since Kevin had been killed she had managed to tell someone without her eyes filling with tears and her voice trembling. Yet still this man hadn't taken the hint that she didn't want to talk to him any more.

'Too bad.' Much to her relief, he didn't pretend to console her on her loss. 'When did it happen?'

'Nearly a year ago.'

'Is that why you left England?' he said shrewdly.

'Yes. How did you guess?'

'It's what I'd have done if it had happened to me. A change of scene, change of people is the best way to go about healing a wound like that.' He gave her a strangely speculative, underbrowed glance. 'I guess you're pretty well over it by now,' he murmured.

She thought about that. He was right again. She was pretty well over the loss. The past ten months, sailing across the ocean and then settling into her job on this island, had done wonders for the state of her emotions and nerves. She was almost back to being as she had been before Kevin's death. But not quite. Now she had a few reservations about falling in love again and getting married.

'I suppose I am,' she murmured and having found the frying-pan at last, added, 'Have you decided? Are you going to share my supper?'

'Not tonight, thanks. After being away from the island for a couple of years I'd like to look up some old friends and dine with them. Is Jilly the only name you have?'

'Yes, it is. Why?'

'Sounds like some sort of candy,' he mocked. 'I'll have to find some other name for you.'

'It's short for Gillian,' she said primly.

'That's even worse,' he remarked with a grimace of distaste. Taking a couple of steps towards her, he reached out a hand and ruffled her hair then smiled down into her eyes. Again her knees wobbled. 'I think I'll call you Blondie,' he murmured, his mouth taking on a taunting slant as if he knew such a nickname would annoy her. 'I'll be back late so don't bother to wait up for me,' was his next aggravating remark. 'See you around, Blondie.'

And, putting his empty beer can down on the counter by the sink, he walked out of the kitchen and the house.

Alone in the kitchen, Jilly swore to herself as she sliced tender chicken meat. All her peace of mind had been shattered because this house, in which she had enjoyed living so much for the past month, had been invaded by a handsome annoying male. Would she have been so disturbed if the invader had been female? The point was worthy of consideration. She faced up to it and had to admit that it wasn't just because he was male that Ed Forster had rattled her. It was because he attracted her physically in a way no other man had ever done, not even Kevin. At their first meeting too! Surely she wasn't going to fall in love with him?

Perhaps she should leave, pack up and go, look for somewhere else to stay. The problem was where and at a rent she could afford. Tomorrow. Like Scarlett O'Hara, she would think about it tomorrow. Right now a shower was in order to sluice away the sweat and the problems of the day while the dinner cooked.

In spite of her determination to put the problem of Edouard Forster out of her mind she didn't sleep at all well, waking that night every hour, so it seemed, to wonder if he had returned to the house. Towards dawn she fell into a heavy sleep only to be rudely awakened an hour later by the sound of the alarm clock pinging. Feeling like a piece of chewed string she blundered into the kitchen to put on coffee then blundered back to the bathroom to have a quick cold shower.

Coffee, hot and black and sinful, did much to revive her, and after munching a croissant filled with jam she left the house, dressed in a crisp, short white skirt of white cotton and a cotton top, V-necked and sleeveless, striped in red, white, blue and green.

The sight of the grey car parked close to her car reminded her that she had a problem to solve and she sighed. Edouard Forster had come back at God-alone-knew what hour of the morning and was now sleeping, not caring at all about how he had wrecked her night. Glancing up at the window of the bedroom in the west wing, she made a face at it and shook her fist. She hoped he had had a rotten dinner last night and that his friends hadn't been as welcoming as he had hoped. Then she got into her car, turned on the engine, revved it long and loud in the hopes of waking him up and then reversed fast and noisily, tearing up the gravel, as he had done last night, before shooting down the drive at high speed.

Distances on the island were never great, since it was only about eight miles wide and eleven miles long, but in order to get from the peninsula where the house was situated to the boatyard where she worked Jilly had to drive from the French side to the Dutch side, a journey which could take either twenty minutes or an hour depending on the state of the roads, the traffic or whatever other man-made disaster occurred to cause a detour or a blockage.

That morning the weather was good, sunny and sparkling. Against the clear blue sky the pointed hills curving round the stretch of water known as the lagoon glowed green. Tiny waves stirred up by the trade wind ruffled the surface of the lagoon making the yachts anchored in it swing at their moorings. As she drove over the swing bridge that spanned the entrance to the lagoon from the sea, Jilly glanced sideways at the Caribbean Sea.

Brilliantly blue, crested by white waves, it seemed to beckon, inviting her to go sailing and to probe its distant violet-blue horizon.

It was mornings like this one that always made her glad she had stayed on this island and it had been on a morning like this that she had first seen the green hills from the deck of the *Artemis*, Reg Turner's yacht, seven months ago. Of all the islands she had visited while crewing on Reg's yacht she had liked this one best, not that it was any more beautiful than Martinique or Antigua, but because on shore she had met so many young people like herself, all searching for a way to make new lives for themselves, nearly all driven there either by lack of opportunity in their own countries or because, like her, they wanted to turn their backs on distress and unhappiness and to start over again.

How grateful she would always be to Reg and Dora Turner for inviting her to come with them partly as a crew member and partly to be a companion to their teenage daughter Julie. The weeks at sea, most of them amazingly storm-free as the ketch had run down the old trade route from the Canary Islands to the West Indies, had been more than beneficial. Away from everything associated with Kevin and their brief year-long marriage, Jilly had gradually recovered from the shock of his death. The company of the other members of the crew had helped too. None of them had known Kevin and none of them had been much concerned by the knowledge that she had been so recently bereaved. Chosen as much for their good humour as for their strength and ability to sail a yacht, they had accepted her casually, as one of the crew.

By the time they had reached St Mark's she had been in good trim. Reg had invited her to go on with him and his family to the States and she probably would have gone with him if Pieter Block hadn't offered her a job. He had been looking for someone to make sails for some time. When she had learned how much he would pay her and had compared it with what she would have earned in England she had accepted the offer immediately. She had imposed on Reg's hospitality long enough. The time had come for her to stand on her own two feet again, to start life all over again, and why not start again on this beautiful tropical island?

So far she had had no regrets, she thought, as she drove slowly up a steep hill in the queue of morning rush-hour traffic. In spite of the occasional frustrations caused by living in a small community where the native islanders had an easy-going attitude to life, she had enjoyed the past months and had made several friends among the cosmo-politan group of people who worked in the boatyard, at the marina, as crews on the charter yachts and catamarans, and in the other small businesses of Williamsburg and also in Caracet, the capital of the French side.

Thinking of friends reminded her of Irma Stratton and thinking of Irma reminded her of Ed Forster again. How handsome he was, to her way of thinking, and yet not a bit like his sister Michelle, who was petite and very French-looking. He had a sense of humour too and she found she was looking forward to meeting him again. She made a guess at his age. Probably about thirty-five. So what was he doing sailing about alone? Why wasn't he married and settled down?

At the top of the hill there was the usual breathtaking view of Town Bay, jade green and gold this morning, dotted with yachts and a few ships, and then she was plunging with the rest of the traffic down towards the outskirts of the town. Once on the by-pass road that curved beside the salt pond and behind the old, original, narrow shopping streets of the town, the traffic lessened and soon she was turning right on to the road that led to the boatyard and the two marinas where the charter boats tied up.

Palm trees rustled in the morning breeze as she walked from the parking area just within the wire fence that separated the boatyard from the narrow roadway. She dodged under the bows of hauled-out yachts and leapt across puddles left by the previous night's rain on her way to the long, grey building on the edge of the water where the ship's chandlery and sail-loft were located. Nearby the travel-lift was busy hauling a big trimaran out of the water. As she reached out a hand to open the door of the office it swung open and Piet Block, her employer, big-shouldered and tow-haired, came out.

'Morning, Jilly,' he roared. Piet always roared at people. 'You're early for once.'

'I'm never late,' she retorted. It was the same routine every morning. He always accused everyone of being late just because they all arrived after he did. 'Who owns the blue trimaran?'

'Belongs to a friend of mine, Ed Forster. He's from the French side of the island. You might have read about him in the yachting magazines. He was third in last year's single-handed race from Plymouth to Newport. It's good to have him back here. Have you finished the awning for the Sunrise Beach Hotel?'

'It's finished.'

'Good. Then we will take it over. Be ready about ten to go with me to fit it. We'll get Hans to give us lunch over there. Part of the deal for getting the awning done on time for him.'

'OK.'

Part of the fun of working for Piet was having the opportunity to go to different places on the island with him to visit clients, and the outing to Sunrise Beach Hotel turned out to be one of the better trips. When she and Piet and Matt, one of the labourers who worked at the boatyard, had finished fitting the orange, white and green awning over the entrance to the main building of the beach resort, they were invited by Hans to swim, either from the perfect beach of shimmering sand or in the pool, and then were entertained to lunch by him in the open-air dining-room overlooking the beach.

Much to Jilly's surprise part of the conversation between her employer and Hans concerned Ed Forster.

'Ed is back,' Piet announced laconically.

'Good. How is he?'

'Seems in good shape,'

'He'll be staying at the House of the Doves, I suppose,' murmured Hans and Jilly tensed all over. Piet knew she was living in that house. Was he going to say something to her about Ed in front of Hans and Matt, ask her if she had met Ed yet?

'Yes, we hauled his boat this morning. He's going to stay around for a while, I'm glad to say,' said Piet, without a glance in her direction.

'It's about time,' said Hans drily. 'He's played about long enough.'

'It hasn't all been play,' retorted Piet. 'Getting ready for those long single-handed races is hard work and the racing itself isn't easy. As I see it his success in that boat of his, that he designed and built himself, is good publicity for the business. We could get orders for more or similar yachts. In fact a couple of the syndicates owning boats he raced against have shown interest in his designs and I'm hopeful at least one of them is going to have their next trimaran built here. Ed would stay here to supervise the construction of it.'

'Then I wish you luck,' said Hans. 'If you can get him to stay anywhere a long time you'll have achieved a miracle.'

On the drive back to the boatyard along a road that resembled a roller-coaster and twisted through the thick bush of banana palms, tall cacti plants and other shrubs of which Jilly did not yet know the names, she wondered whether to mention to Piet that she had already met Ed Forster or whether to wait until he brought the subject up. In the end she decided to wait for him to mention Ed, but by the time they arrived back at the boatyard he hadn't.

Much to her surprise, Ed was in the office talking to Marcha, Piet's woman friend and business partner. They were both studying a catalogue of yachting equipment. As he looked up Ed glanced straight at Jilly and smiled. Her legs did their wobbling trick.

'Jilly, I guess you have already met Ed so I won't bother to introduce you,' said Marcha, in her gruff Dutch-accented voice.

'Yes, we've met.' Jilly managed to speak coolly. 'Excuse me, I have work to do.' With a polite nod in Ed's direction she went through to the store-room behind the office and climbed the ladder up to the sail-loft.

She didn't see Ed again that day, although she half hoped he would come up to the sail-loft to talk to her and later hoped he would be in the house when she arrived there. But

his car wasn't in the parking-place and by the time she had
gone to bed he hadn't returned. Next morning he was still
in his wing of the house, presumably asleep, when she left
for work, and although she saw him examining the hulls of
his trimaran in the boatyard later that day and he was in
the office with Piet when she passed through once, he didn't
even raise his head to look at her and made no attempt to
visit her in her loft.

So why should she care if he ignored her? Wasn't it better
that way? Safer? she argued with herself as she drove back
to the house in the short sunset time. But she couldn't help
feeling disappointed when there was no grey car parked in
the parking-space under the poinciana trees or when he
hadn't returned by the time she had finished her supper.
She suspected he was out with friends again. Or with a
friend. A woman friend, probably. A French woman who
would be more to his taste. Why should she care who he was
with? He meant nothing to her. He might like the colour of
her hair but otherwise she just wasn't his type, she was too
young and inexperienced. He had said so.

To stop thinking about him she left the house and drove
out to visit some friends who lived near the airport and
didn't return until after midnight. To her smug satisfaction
the grey car was back. But no lights glowed in the windows
of the rooms in the west wing and there was no sign of Ed in
the living-rooms or kitchen. He had gone to bed.

Next day being Saturday she worked only in the
morning and, after lunch with some friends at one of the
local restaurants, she did some shopping and drove back to
the house. When she saw Ed's car she felt a little spurt of
excitement. Then she saw the other car, a Peugeot. He had
a visitor. Possibly the woman she had suspected him of

visiting every evening since he had arrived, she thought waspishly.

Disappointment swamped the feeling of excitement and was followed by irritation when she heard voices as she approached the pool terrace at the front of the house. Under the bright afternoon sun the reddish tiles of the apron glowed warmly and the limpid pool glinted with many reflected colours. Seeing that there were several people including Ed lounging in deck-chairs beside the pool, Jilly tried to go past them towards the front door without being observed, only to find her way blocked by Ed who had sprung from his chair.

'Nice to see you home so early,' he said and she raised her gaze from his broad naked chest to his eyes, so vividly blue between their short black lashes. 'We're having a poolside party. Won't you join us?'

She glanced sideways. Three women and two men, two of the women sleek-skinned, wearing bikinis, the other one slightly older, shapely in a one-piece bathing-suit. The two men were both middle-aged. One of them had white hair. All were chattering in French. The poolside table was littered with empty glasses.

CHAPTER TWO

To Jilly's disappointed, irritated eyes the group around the pool looked as if they were holding an orgy. Averting her glance she tried to pass Ed. He side-stepped to block her way again.

'No, thanks,' she said stiffly, staring woodenly at his bare chest.

'Don't be shy,' he mocked and for some reason that annoyed her even more. She glared up at him.

'I'm not shy,' she said loudly and clearly. 'I'm just particular about the company I keep. Excuse me.'

She pushed past him, ran up the steps into the house and went straight to her room. She would go swimming from the beach rather than join Ed Forster and his sleazy friends at the poolside. After changing into a swimsuit of purple and green stripes, she left the house by one of the long windows in the east wing, and by taking a path through the shrubbery, found her way to the narrow sandy path that slanted down from the main road to the beach that rimmed Baie Jaune, a wide indentation in the coastline.

The beach was partially private, for the use only of the residents of the big houses that hid among the trees on the cliffs. The rock of the cliffs was ochre-coloured and the sand was the same colour, thick and coarse-grained. Surf beat against the shore, white lacy foam leaping up from the jade-green rollers that were surging in. Beyond the surge the sea was a different colour, almost deep purple except where the sunlight bleached it to azure. In the distance the small island of Angosta was merely a dark blue line on the horizon.

There was no one on the beach. Jilly had it all to herself. For a while she played in the surf then she lay on her towel after smoothing strong sun-lotion on her skin. She tried to read the blockbuster she had brought with her but her thoughts would keep straying to Ed Forster and her own strange reaction to his invitation to join his poolside party.

Her rudeness, she realised, had sprung directly from her disappointment at finding him not alone. She had behaved as if he were hers, as if he were her boyfriend, her lover, her husband; as if he were a possession of hers. Why?

She wasn't normally over-possessive about people. She enjoyed her own freedom too much to be like that. Although she had loved Kevin very much she had never acted possessively with him, had never objected to his friends being around just as he had never objected to her friends being around. So why should she feel possessive about a man she had only just met and whom she wasn't sure she even liked?

She had to admit she found him extremely attractive, she thought as she laid her head down on her folded arms and closed her eyes. And she was getting used to the idea of sharing the house with him. It was nice to know he was there in the night, not always all night it was true, but there part of the time, close at hand, to be called on for help if the necessity arose.

Which one of those sleek golden-skinned French women was his, she wondered? If she had stayed and had joined the party she would have found out, wouldn't she? And then she would have been able to take the woman's measure.

Heavens, what was she thinking about? It was unlike her to indulge in fantasy. Perhaps she had been without a man too long. Since Kevin had been killed she hadn't been interested at all in sex, although there had been men interested in having sex with her. Simon, for instance. A member of Reg's crew, he had been very interested in her, but in her numbed and frozen widowed state she had found it easy to keep him at a distance.

Where was he now? In the last letter she had received from Dora Turner there had been a mention of Simon. He had left the Turners in Florida, intending to help deliver a yacht from there to Australia for its owner and hoping one day to return to the West Indies. Any day now he might turn up at the boatyard. It always fascinated her the way the same people turned up on the island, young men and women who made their livings sailing other people's boats.

'You're beginning to burn,' Edouard Forster said, quite close to her.

Surprised, she lifted her head and opened her eyes. He was sitting on the sand beside her and nothing could have been colder than the expression in his eyes. She sat up turning to face the sun, uncomfortably aware that once again he was right, the skin on her back was beginning to burn. On the edge of the surf two of the young women from his party were playing, rushing in and out of the breakers, shrieking when the undertow caught them and flung them ashore again. They looked much younger than they had on the pool terrace, more like teenagers.

'They're my cousin Alicia's twin daughters, from France. They are on holiday here with her and her husband René, staying with my grandfather, my mother's father who still lives in retirement in Caracet,' he said. 'I'd have introduced you to them all if you'd condescended to join us at the poolside.' His voice was cold too, chiding her for her abrupt rudeness.

Mortified, she couldn't look at him, only past him at the three figures approaching along the beach, a woman and two men. One of the men, the one with white hair, walked slowly and leaned on the arm of the other man.

'I'm sorry I was rude,' she muttered. 'You see, I thought that ...'

'Don't bother to make excuses,' he interrupted her bitingly. 'I know what you thought. You saw three women in swimsuits, some glasses and jumped to conclusions. The wrong ones. Orgies aren't my style. In spite of what you might hear to the contrary.'

That made her look right at him. There was the suspicion of a smile lurking in the blue eyes now, warming them with little dancing sparks of light. He leaned towards her until his head was almost touching hers. She smelt the salty tang of his skin, the muskiness of his thick hair and felt desire coil within her when his breath wafted across her cheek.

'A black sheep's reputation is always made out to be worse than it actually is,' he said. 'When I was younger I was a little wild, given to holding riotous beach parties here on the island, but that was a long time ago, before I ran away with another guy's wife.'

Round-eyed she swayed back a little, away from the magnetic pull of his attraction, staring at him disbelievingly.

'Aren't you ever serious?' she croaked.

'Often, and never more so than I am now. For some reason that I can't quite fathom I want you to know the truth about me. I also want you to meet my relatives.' He glanced over his shoulder at the approaching threesome and twisted agilely to his feet. He held out a hand to her and after a slight hesitation she put hers in it and let him help her up. Still holding her hand he led her forward to meet the two men and the woman. He addressed them in rapid

French and she heard her own name. Then turning to her he said in English,

'Jill, I would like you to meet my grandfather, Jules Martin, and also my cousin Alicia and her husband René Dumont.'

'I'm pleased to meet you,' Jilly said politely, wishing she had paid more attention to her French lessons when she had attended school.

Jules Martin, who had dark brown eyes set in a network of fine wrinkles, was the only one who spoke.

'We are pleased to meet you too, *madame*,' he said in strongly accented English. 'Edouard must bring you to visit me when you are both in the town.' Mischievous humour flickered suddenly in his wise old eyes as he glanced at Ed. 'You make a good choice this time. I approve. Maybe you settle down now, eh?'

'Maybe,' replied Ed evasively and said something in French.

The old man answered him with an affectionate grin before turning away to say something to the others. Jilly tugged at Ed's hand. He looked down at her.

'What did your grandfather mean?' she whispered. 'What have you been telling them about me?'

'Only that we are both living in the house,' he replied with a wicked grin. 'Can I help it if they also jump to conclusions.'

'You devil.' She pulled her hand out of his grasp and turned to Jules Martin. '*Monsieur*, you must understand that when Ed says he and I are both living in your granddaughter's house he doesn't mean that we . . . that he and I are living together.'

The old man's thick eyebrows went up in a familiar derisive way.

'No? Not yet? Then all I can say is that you are losing

your touch, Ed,' he remarked drily. 'It seems that René and Allie are ready to leave,' he went on, looking after the couple who were now walking with the two girls in the direction of the path that led to main road. '*Au revoir, madame.* Do not forget now. Come and visit me in Caracet.'

Taking hold of Ed's arm he began to walk after the others and Jilly was left to stare after them, raging inwardly at the trick Ed had played on her. Somehow she had to get back at him for it. Perhaps the best way would be to move out before the news was spread all through the yachting community on the island that she was Ed Forster's latest mistress.

She didn't follow Ed, his grandfather and the others immediately, but went for another swim in the surf, diving into each breaker as it approached her and floating up in the calm surface between the crests until she was quite a long way from the beach. Returning was both exhilarating and a little wild and she wished she had been on a surfboard. The water seemed to grab her and hurl her forward, causing her to lose her breath entirely and to sink downwards often. As she got nearer to the beach she knew that she was in real danger of being caught by the fierce undertow and of being flung like a drowned rat on the shore. That did in fact happen and, blinded by salt water, choking and spluttering, she crashed in a heap on the sand, her bare skin scratched, her hair wet and straggling, her swimsuit ripped and all her breath gone.

The weight of another breaker crashing down on top of her alerted her. Struggling to her feet, she staggered up the beach away from the surf and flopped down again exhausted, aware that the sun was slipping down in the west and that the shadows of the cliffs were beginning to cool the sand. The tide had advanced up the beach and now there was only a narrow strand of sand left between the sea

and the cliffs. If she didn't go soon, before the water reached
the foot of the cliffs, she would either be drowned or would
have to save herself by climbing the sheer face of the cliffs.

Again she struggled to her feet. Her towel and her book
had been washed away long ago. Still staggering a little,
her hand pressed to her ribs where she hurt whenever she
breathed, she began to walk along, sometimes through the
water spreading over the sand from yet another breaker,
sometimes clambering over the rocks at the foot of the cliffs.
At last she reached the sandy pathway, her feet sinking into
the softness. A few more yards and she was on the driveway
leading to the house, the stones of the gravel piercing the
soles of her bare feet.

The swimming-pool was dappled with golden sunset
light and the shadows of wind-ruffled trees. The deck-
chairs were deserted and the glasses had gone from the
tables. In the house was no sound yet she knew Ed must be
somewhere because his car was still in the parking-space.
She was glad he wasn't around. She wanted to get to her
bedroom and close the door, be alone for an hour or two
while she recovered from her breathtaking experience,
examined her scratched skin and stripped off her torn
swimsuit. If he saw her in a bedraggled state he would
probably guess what had happened to her and would have
something caustic to say.

She made the mistake of looking into the living-room. He
was there, lounging on the settee, a half-empty glass of some
liquor or other on the table beside him. She tried to
withdraw noiselessly and collided with a chair behind her.
Its legs screeched on the tiled floor. He looked up, his eyes
flashing like blue lightning in the dim shape of his face. He
rose to his feet in one lithe movement.

'Good God, what happened to you?' he exclaimed. In a
couple of strides he was beside her, his big hands seizing her

bare chilled shoulders as he pulled her closer to him so that he could peer at her face in the fast-fading light.

'Nothing,' she lied, and her teeth betrayed her by chattering. Suddenly she was shivering from head to foot with reaction.

'Like hell it was nothing,' he growled. 'You've been in the surf, haven't you? You were caught in the undertow. You bloody fool! Haven't you more sense than to go swimming alone in that surf?'

Strangely enough his rebuke, instead of rousing her to retaliation, reduced her to tears.

'You don't have to be so rough,' she sobbed. 'Or so concerned. I don't need your concern. Now let me go. I'm going to bed. All I need is a rest. I'll be all right, honestly.' Since he didn't seem to be doing what she had asked but was still holding her by the shoulders, she raised her voice and shouted, 'Let me go!'

He obliged immediately and contrarily she wished he hadn't because she missed the warmth and strength of his grasp, needed his support in fact, because she swayed suddenly and, staggering backwards, collapsed in the chair behind her. Tears poured down her face and she covered it with her hands, moaning a little in her distress, as long shivers shook her from head to foot.

He moved quickly, hauling her out of the chair and scooping her up in his arms, carrying her from the living-room and along the passage to her bedroom, kicking the door open. He strode in and deposited her on the bed. While she gulped for breath, her throat and gullet raw from having swallowed so much salt water, he pulled the thin blanket from beneath her and threw it on top of her.

'Stay there. Don't you dare move. I'll be back,' he ordered crisply and left the room.

Slowly she stopped crying and wiped her face on a

corner of the sheet that was under her. She was still shaking but warmth from the blanket was beginning to penetrate through her damp skin and beneath her the mattress felt soft but supportive. She thought of Ed's order as he had left the room. She had no intention of moving. Not now. Not tonight. Tomorrow maybe. Tomorrow she would leave, find some other accommodation. She couldn't possibly stay in this house while he was living in it, not after this afternoon's embarrassing events.

'Jill.' She stiffened in surprise. No one ever called her Jill. 'Sit up. If you can.'

Turning her head she looked up at him. He seemed huge to her as he towered above the bed. In his hand he held a glass. She struggled into a sitting position. One strap of her swimsuit slipped down. The bodice sagged, revealing one pink-tipped breast. He seemed to be very interested in the shape of it, so with fingers that still trembled slightly she managed to find the strap and pull it up over her shoulder.

'Never mind that,' he said brusquely and the edge of the bed sank beneath his weight as he sat down on it. 'Drink this.'

'What is it?'

'Cognac.'

'I don't want it. What are you trying to do? Make me drunk?'

'Sure I am,' he agreed easily. 'I want you as high as a kite and then you won't notice when I slip into your bed and take advantage of you during the night,' he scoffed. 'What in hell has happened to you during your short life to make you so damned prickly and so suspicious of a guy? Your late lamented do this to you?'

'Of course not. Kevin was kind and gentle. It's just that you . . .' She broke off, not knowing how to describe the effect he had on her and then not wanting him to know he had an effect on her.

'OK, message received. It's just me you're suspicious of.' He glanced down at the glass in his hand and frowned. 'It's all I can think of to give you. You scared the hell out of me in there, coming in with your swimsuit all torn and your hair like yellow seaweed hanging about your pale face. You looked like a ghost.' His glance flashed up to her face and leaned towards her. 'You're still white.' He raised his free hand and stroked a finger down one of her cheeks while his eyes looked right into hers.

His touch was like a hot iron burning her skin. He shouldn't have touched her, she thought hazily. He was breaking the ground-rule she had laid down. Hands off, she had told him. She should remind him but she couldn't speak nor could she move. Mesmerising her with the intensely blue stare of his eyes, he continued to break the rule and let his fingers slide down her cheek over the line of her jaw to her throat, then drift down to the cleft between her breasts. And she let him do it because she found she wanted him to touch her. To hell with her own ground-rules.

She raised her head from the pillow so that her face was close to his. From under drooping eyelids she saw the wickedly humorous curve of his lips come closer to hers, saw them part sensually. Then they were against hers. Back against the pillow she sank, her lips parting to welcome the hard, hot probe of his tongue. His kiss was hungry and demanding but it was comforting too, putting the shock she had received to retreat, warming her and convincing her that she was alive and kicking. It coaxed her to respond and she did willingly, enjoying the taste of his tongue and lips, the heat of his mouth, the silky feel of his hair under her hands, the roughness of his bare chest against her half-covered breasts.

The cognac glass crashed to the tiled floor and she

laughed silently at his muffled curse spoken against her lips, but he didn't move away to pick up the pieces. Instead he managed somehow to shift her over on the bed so that he could lie beside her, still claiming her lips with his. Then for a while there was no sound in that room except that of their heavy breathing, and no movement except that of their hands stroking and titillating.

'I didn't intend this to happen right now so soon after you'd nearly drowned,' he whispered against her cheek when they both came up for air. Both of them under the blanket now they seemed to be wrapped in a warm cocoon of their own making, their legs entwined. 'I want you,' he whispered and kissed her again.

'But only because you haven't had anyone in a long time,' she gasped when he gave her a chance to speak.

'Maybe,' he murmured, lifting lazy fingers through strands of her drying hair. 'But I was going to wait until you stopped being prickly and suspicious, until you were more friendly. And I'm going to wait now until you've had that rest you said you would have.' He began to slide away from her.

'Oh.' Disappointment welled up within her. 'That isn't fair,' she complained.

'What do you mean, not fair?' he said rolling back to her.

'It isn't fair of you to make love to me like you did just now and then leave me.' Suddenly shy she hid her face in the smooth bulk of his shoulder. 'I want you too,' she whispered, facing up to the truth at last, to the reality of her own need.

'But only because you haven't had anyone in a long time,' he joked gently. 'Not since Kevin, is my guess. Would I be right?'

'You would be right,' she said with a sigh. 'I'm beginning to think you're one of those aggravating men who are always right,' she teased.

'Not always. Just mostly right,' he retorted with a grin. 'You know, even in a half-drowned state you're attractive, with your milk-white skin, golden eyes and flaxen hair, flaxen when it's dry that is. It's nearly dry now and it feels like silk, and so does your skin.' He looked into her eyes, his own dark and lustful. 'I can't stay this close to you any longer without making love to you, but only if it's what you want, Jill.'

'I want it,' she whispered.

He made no response other than to kiss her again. Her eyes closed and she seemed to whirl in a hot darkness. Beneath his weight her bones melted. She sank into the mattress, all her feelings rushing together to create a knot of desire low down in her body, a knot that could only be released in one way and by him. Clinging to him, inciting him with subtle movements of her hips, she gave no thought as to whether it was right or wrong. It was something she had to do there and then with him and only him. He had stepped into her life just when she had been longing for someone like him to appear and she had to make the most of his presence because she had learned the hard way that life often ends abruptly. It had ended for Kevin like that. It had almost ended for her on the beach that afternoon.

Passion flamed between them instantly. It was as if they had been made for each other and had been coming to that place and point in time for many years, travelling different roads on a long journey that had ended at last in a lovers' meeting. Almost desperately they caressed each other as the tropical darkness swooped into the room enfolding them with its sensuous warmth.

'I guess this is better than cognac as a cure.' Ed said it rather breathlessly, his lips moving against her throat as they both approached the point of no return.

'Much better,' she breathed from the depths of a dark sensuousness.

To her surprise and distress he stiffened and shifted away from her, breaking out of the circle of her arms that had been curved around him. Her eyes flew open. Without the warmth of his hard muscular body, without its weight, she felt suddenly chilled, all desire draining from her.

'What is it? What's the matter?' she whispered.

In the purple darkness of the room he was a darker shape, looming over her.

'What about that ground-rule of yours, the one you laid down the other night?' he said.

Somehow she had to get him back into her arms, to press close to him again. Her eager fingers found and caressed the hard clean line of his jaw, drifting like feathers over his skin.

'I only made that rule because I was afraid of what happened to me when we met the other night,' she murmured. Having found his lips she raised herself in the bed so that she could kiss them, but he turned his head and her lips brushed his cheek only. 'I was afraid I might fall in love with you,' she added softly, laughing a little at herself. 'A lot of good it was making a rule like that. It didn't help at all. It didn't stop me from falling in love with you after all.'

'Don't say that,' he said in a harsh most un-lover-like way. He rolled away from her and off the bed. She could tell by his movements that he had found his shorts and was pulling them on. Rejected desire lying like a lead weight in the lower part of her body, she sat up, fingers reaching for the bedside lamp. She found the switch and snapped on the light. In the loom of the light his face looked as if it were carved from teak. Shivering a little she draped the blanket about her.

'Why shouldn't I say it?' she answered. 'It's true. I tried

hard not to but it's happened. I have fallen in love with you.
I know I have because I've been wanting you to make love
to me,' she tried to explain. 'You see, I can't make love
unless I'm in love. That's how I know. I can't do it with
someone I'm not particularly attracted to. I don't think you
can, either.'

Groaning with exasperation he raked his tousled hair,
paced half-way to the doorway as if he intended to leave the
room and then paced back again to frown down at her.

'I knew it. I felt it in my bones that you're too young, too
inexperienced to have an affair with someone like me,' he
muttered through taut lips. He sat down again on the edge
of the bed and leaned towards her. 'I have to tell you I don't
believe in this falling-in-love bit. Once, years ago when I
was young and didn't know any better, I believed in it, but
it didn't take me long to find out it's all a snare and a
delusion.' His voice grated bitterly. 'By then I'd made some
people of whom I was very fond extremely unhappy and
had destroyed the peace of mind of a man who had never
done me any harm.'

'You're talking about the time you eloped with a married
woman,' she guessed.

'Am I?' His lips twisted cynically. 'You'd just love to
know the whole story, wouldn't you, so that you could
romanticise it? Well, you're not going to hear it right now.
What happened years ago is past history, a mistake I made
and from which I learned that love is something women
deal in, something they use to get their own way. So if you
want to continue with what we've begun this afternoon,
don't ever say you're in love with me. Don't even think it.'

'Oh, I don't understand you,' she complained.

'Then don't try. Just accept what it is I can offer you
while we're both living in this house and make the most of
it. There is something between us—you feel it and I feel it

and at first we both tried to deny that we were attracted to each other, that the age-old chemistry was working again between a woman and a man. We'd have got together sooner or later during the next couple of weeks. Your little accident this afternoon precipitated things, that's all.'

'I'm not sure that I can accept what it is you can offer,' she muttered, avoiding his steady gaze. 'Oh, I know it's done all the time these days. Couples live together without being married. Most of my friends on this island do. But I can't do it unless I'm in love with the other person or believe I'm in love with him.'

'Well, I understand that. You're a romantic. So we'll leave it there,' he said coolly. 'And we'll carry on as if nothing had happened this evening, as if I'd never touched you and you had never touched me. It was just a flare-up, a flash-fire that nearly got out of control, and was brought on by propinquity. I'll try to keep out of your way. I don't want to be responsible for hurting you.'

'No, no.' The words seemed to be torn from her throat. Her arms reached out to him. 'I don't want you to do that. I want to see you every day. I want you to be here in the house when I leave in the morning, to see you at the boatyard sometimes. Oh, why did you have to touch me, kiss me? Why couldn't we have waited?' she wailed.

'I guess you went to my head because I haven't been with anyone for a while, as you put it so accurately,' he replied with a gruff laugh. 'Do you know when Michelle is coming back?'

'At the end of April. If she's finished filming by then.'

'So we have nearly three months to enjoy each other's company, if I stay on.'

'I'm still not sure I can do what you ask,' she said shakily. 'I don't share your attitude to love because my own experience has been different. I loved Kevin and he loved me. We told each other we did before we married. We couldn't either of us have lived together with or without marriage if we hadn't been in love with each other, so I'm not sure I can indulge in an illicit relationship with you without ... without being in love with you.' She clung to him suddenly, her arms about him. 'You must be a little bit in love with me,' she whispered urgently, her lips tasting the salty tang of his skin as they moved against his shoulder. 'You said you like the way I look. You were concerned when you knew I'd been knocked down by the undertow and you tried to care for me. You said just now you didn't want me to be hurt so that means you love me just a little bit. Why won't you admit it as I have that we have fallen in love with each other, against our wills, admittedly, but even so ...?'

'Jill,' he was whispering hoarsely when another voice, a female voice, sang out in the passage way,

'Jilly? Where are you? We're all here. Oohoo. Are you in the loo?'

'Who the hell is it?' growled Ed, pushing away from her and getting to his feet.

'Oh, help!' Jilly sat up, clutching the blanket about her. 'I'd forgotten. I asked some friends over for supper this evening.'

'Then I'd better go and make them welcome while you get dressed,' he said and went towards the door.

'Ed. Come back. They don't know you're living here too.' she gasped.

'No?' He turned to look at her. Devilry danced in his eyes and curled his lips. 'Then they're about to find out, aren't they? Want me to send them away, tell them you're not up to entertaining?'

'No. Do you have to go that way? Couldn't you leave by the patio window in the next room and walk round to your wing? That way they won't see you.'

'Ashamed of me? Aren't I good enough for your friends?' he jeered.

'Jilly! Where are you?' The woman's voice was much nearer now and Jilly recognised it as belonging to Ruth Burrows.

But before she could call out an answer Ed left the room and stepped out into the passage. Before he closed the door behind him she heard him say, 'Hi, Ruth. This is a not-so-pleasant surprise.'

Tossing back the thin blanket, Jilly swung off the bed, but she had hardly grabbed her dressing-gown from the chair on to which she had thrown it that morning when the door opened and Ruth barged into the room.

CHAPTER THREE

'JILLY, are you all right? Ed said you were resting after an accident. What happened?'

Ruth Burrows, who was Jilly's closest friend on the island, was also from England. She had been first mate and crew on one of the catamarans that ferried tourists to and from the neighbouring French island of Monteux for nearly four years and lived, without the blessing of marriage, with Raoul Savard, the captain of the catamaran.

'Nothing much,' Jilly said coolly, tying the belt of her dressing-gown as she turned to face Ruth. 'I went swimming in the surf and got caught by the undertow. It knocked me down on the beach, took all my breath away, made me feel really strange.'

'That's all?' squeaked Ruth. 'You could have drowned. Swimming in that on a windy day like this. Haven't you got any sense?'

'Apparently not,' said Jilly drily, thinking of Ed's more forceful rebuke.

Built on generous lines, as muscular as any man, Ruth advanced further into the room, her bright glance flicking curiously over Jilly's appearance.

'Except for the state of your hair you don't look as if you've been half drowned,' she murmured. 'In fact . . .' she broke off frowning, then demanded sharply, 'What's Ed Forster doing in this house? I thought you were living here alone, looking after it for Michelle Martin.'

Jilly hesitated fractionally before replying. No point in lying to Ruth now that she had seen Ed and seemed to know who he was.

'He arrived yesterday. He's Michelle's brother. She forgot to tell Irma Stratton he would be coming.'

'You mean he's going to live in the house while you're living in it?' exclaimed Ruth.

'Yes,' replied Jilly, surprised at how cool she felt. She had told the truth and didn't care what Ruth thought about it. Why should she? She was an adult and what she did in private was her own business. 'Please will you tell the others I won't be long? I must take a shower and rinse the salt off. You might ask Raoul to get the barbecue going. It's gas-fired and is already out by the pool. Did you bring the rolls and the salad stuff?'

'Everything is under control,' replied Ruth rather tersely and sat down suddenly on the edge of the bed as if the strength had left her legs. 'I'm absolutely amazed!' she gasped. 'To think that you, of all the women I know on this island, are living in this house with Ed Forster!'

'I'm not living with him,' Jilly snapped defensively. 'Just because he's here in the house, you're not to think he and I are living together.'

'Knowing Ed's reputation with women, what else can anyone think?' jeered Ruth, rolling her eyes. 'Have you any idea what you've taken on? The whole island knows about him and his affairs. Like father like son, they all say. You know who his father was, don't you?'

'No, I don't. I don't know anything about him other than that he is Michelle's brother,' retorted Jilly. Except that he's beautiful and strong, honest and compassionate and he's made me feel alive in a way I haven't felt for a long time, her ungovernable, vulnerable heart seemed to sing within her.

'Oh, lord, that makes it even worse,' groaned Ruth, leaning back on the bed supporting herself on her elbows, a position that emphasised her big breasts, taut under the cotton top she was wearing, and the hard shape of her thighs moulded by thin cotton pants. 'Did you ever see any films starring Jon Forster?'

'Yes,' Jilly paused, remembering a handsome actor with intensely blue eyes who had always played 'great lover' roles in sensationally sexy American films.

'Well, Ed Forster is his only son.'

'So?'

'So he's inherited his old man's partiality for the opposite sex. No woman with anything in the way of good looks or a great figure is safe from him and last time he was here he even tried it on with me.' Jilly wondered whether it was her imagination playing tricks, but it seemed to her that Ruth found a certain satisfaction in having been the object of Ed's attentions at some time or other. 'Did you know that Jon Forster was married several times?' Ruth continued.

'No, I didn't,' replied Jilly with a laugh. 'I'm not a film buff and I've never been particularly interested in the private lives of film stars.'

'Pity you haven't. You might have been a bit more leery about Ed, when he showed up,' remarked Ruth drily. Lunging up from the bed, she walked over to the long mirror on the front of the clothes closet and began to push at her short curly brown hair, then to examine her complexion. Looking at Jilly's reflection in the mirror, she added,

'Michelle's and Ed's mother was one of his wives, third or second, I'm not sure which. He met her when he was

vacationing on the island and having this house built. She
was the daughter of a French Government official who still
lives on the island. When she divorced Jon, Ed went to live
with his father in Hollywood.' Ruth swung away from the
mirror and looked around the luxuriously furnished room.
'This house is fabulous and must be worth millions of
dollars, to say nothing of pounds sterling,' she remarked
enviously. 'I wonder if you know how lucky you are to be
living in it.'

'Yes, I do,' said Jilly with a touch of impatience. 'But I'd
like to know, too, how it is you know so much about Ed's
and Michelle's mother and father.'

'I read some of it in movie magazines and then Raoul
confirmed some of it. His mother is from the French side too
and used to know Ed's mother,' replied Ruth airily. 'Raoul
used to go to school with Ed when they were little boys in
Caracet. He knows a lot about Ed, about how wild he was
when he was younger, running off with other men's wives.
Don't have anything to do with him, Jilly. He's dynamite.'

'Oh, Ruth, you are funny.' Jilly managed to sound
scornful. 'You've read so many of those sexy novels that
you're beginning to believe some men want to have sex
with every woman they meet.'

'Then what was Ed doing in this room?' Ruth demanded
bluntly 'You can't deny he was in here with you when I
called to you.'

'No, I can't,' said Jilly with dignity. It seemed to her that
Ruth was suddenly far too nosy, truculent too, almost as if
she resented the fact that Ed had been in the bedroom. As if
she were jealous? 'He was concerned because I'd been
knocked out by the undertow. He brought me something to
drink.'

'And what did you do? Swipe it out of his hand?' Ruth

asked, her glance going to the pieces of glass and the drying
sticky cognac on the tiles. 'There's a way to show your
gratitude for his concern,' she mocked, then returning to
her more serious manner she pleaded, 'I'm only trying to
warn you, love, about him. His reputation stinks. And
you're too good for him. You're right, he is like one of those
men in those trashy novels I read all the time. Don't stay in
this house while he's in it. Keep your distance from him.
And if you don't believe me ask anyone else who knows him
what he's like. Ask Piet. No, better not ask Piet since he and
Ed are good friends. But you could ask Marcha. She should
know all about him. I'm only warning you out of
friendship, Jilly, and because you seem to be a bit naïve
about some things. I wouldn't like you to get hurt.'

'Thanks, I appreciate your concern,' Jilly replied, her
own attitude softening a little. 'But don't worry about me. I
can take care of myself.'

'I wonder if you can. You're such a romantic at heart.
Easy meat for the Don Juans of this world, I'd say. And
you've certainly come up against one in Ed Forster. The
tales I could tell you about him!'

'Don't,' said Jilly sharply. 'At least not right now. There
isn't time. Go out and tell the others I'll be with them as
soon as I can. Go on. I must have a shower and wash my
hair.'

'And wash Ed Forster right out of it?' chanted Ruth with
a sudden sly grin as she got to her feet. 'Go to it, Jilly, love.'

In the shower as she shampooed her hair Jilly thought
over all Ruth had told her about Ed and agreed with her
friend that it would be best if she did wash him out of her
mind and out of her heart. She didn't doubt that there was
probably some truth in Ruth's suggestion that Ed was a
womaniser. Hadn't she sensed that about him herself at

their first meeting? Wasn't that why she had laid down that ground-rule? And hadn't Ed warned her in an oblique sort of way when he had said she was too young, too inexperienced to have an affair with a man like him?

But what fun it would be, an impish voice whispered within her, if she could do it without being hurt and make him fall in love with her before Michelle came back and she had to leave this house.

Amused by her own mischievous thoughts and more than a little surprised by them, she rubbed herself dry quickly, dressed in a shift-like dress of white cotton printed with bright hibiscus blossoms, flicked a comb through her hair which was almost dry and hurried out on to the floodlit terrace.

Pungent smoke from the barbecue drifted lazily away from the pool area and was swallowed up by the darkness. Above the shapes of high palms the sickle moon glittered in a starlit sky. As always the tropical night cast a magical spell over everything, exciting the senses. Music thumping out from the cassette player, brought by someone, sounded more throbbingly exotic. Voices seemed softer, more suggestive. Bare suntanned skin shone more sleekly than in the sunlight, tempting the fingers to touch and caress. Eyes glinted in dark faces, seeming to send erotic messages.

Only half aware of being greeted by her friends, Jilly looked around, searching for Ed and not finding him. He hadn't stayed to join her party any more than she had stayed to join his party that afternoon. He wasn't even with Raoul who was supervising the grilling of the steaks. Suppressing her disappointment because he wasn't there, she helped herself to a glass of white wine from a bottle that Ruth was handing around, and swallowed down half of it in one gulp. Perhaps the wine would help to melt that hard knot of frustration that had coiled in her loins. Perhaps under its heady influence she would forget this new pain that had been inflicted upon her by Ed's withdrawal just when they had both been on the brink of plunging into the maelstrom of passion.

The wine flowed, cans of beer were consumed, someone pushed someone else into the pool and soon nearly everyone was in it, splashing and laughing. The food being ready, Jilly brought a small Chinese gong from the entrance hall of the house and banged on it and they all climbed out of the pool to grab plates and help themselves from the heap of steaks, bowls of salad and rolls of butter.

While they were eating some latecomers arrived, Gerry and Susan Leigh, also from England, who were in the process of cruising around the world on their own yacht but had been on the island almost as long as Jilly had, Gerry working as a carpenter at the boatyard and Susan teaching riding at a riding-school set up by another expatriate Briton. With them was Simon Travis, who had crewed with Jilly on Reg Turner's ketch.

'When did you get here?' asked Jilly after they had hugged each other in delight at meeting again.

'This afternoon.' Not much taller than she was, slightly built but as tough as wire, he was darkly tanned and his brown curly hair was bleached almost as blonde as her own. 'Came on a schooner, from the Virgin Islands. I've been crewing on it, taking out charter parties since the beginning of December, but today I left and came ashore to find you.' He smiled at her. 'It's good to see you, Jilly. How have you been getting on at the boatyard?'

'Fine. I'm not surprised to see you back here. In her last letter Dora said you were hoping to go to Australia, and that was why you left the *Artemis*. Did you go? Have you been there and come back?'

His grey eyes hidden by their heavy lids, Simon looked down at his plate of food and shook his head.

'No. That little idea fell through. The guy who owned the yacht that was being delivered to Australia decided to hire someone as captain who didn't want me as a member of his crew. To cut a long story short, I got a lift up to Maine where I knew that a fellow I'd known in England was captain of one of the charter schooners which sail there in the summer and come south to St Thomas in the winter. He took me on as first mate and I've been with the schooner ever since. Until today, that is. And today I felt it was time for another change so I signed off.' He took a swig of beer and glanced around at the floodlit terrace and then at the shadowy house. 'This is a great place, Jilly. You must be doing well to be able to rent accommodation like this.'

'Oh, I don't rent it. I'm a sort of housekeeper living here rent-free while the owner of the house is in France for a few months. Piet pays me well for what I do but not well enough for me to rent something like this. Accommodation is really hard to get on the island. Where are you going to stay now that you've let the schooner?'

'I hoped to find a bunk on some yacht. Know of anyone who wants their yacht looked after for a while? Or any other job? What about the boatyard? Gerry seems to be doing well there. Any chance of Piet Block employing me?'

'I'm not sure. Gerry will soon have to leave because his time on the island is coming to an end and he isn't doing a job an islander can't do. And Piet isn't keen any more on hiring people who aren't here legally, who are just on visitor's permits. I think he must have been in trouble with the authorities for hiring people like you and Gerry who sail in here hoping to pick up work. That's why he went to so much trouble to have me legalised.' She paused. Someone had turned up the volume on the cassette player and dancing had started. She sensed a tenseness in Simon, a sort of desperation. She had met it before in other young men she had known who were wandering about the world trying to find a niche. For old times' sake she had to try and help him. She turned and smiled at him. 'I'll put in a word for you with Piet, if you like,' she offered.

His sudden smile in return lit up his sun-tanned face with fleeting charm and he bent his head to kiss her cheek in appreciation.

'Thanks, Jilly, I knew you wouldn't let me down,' he whispered.

'Let's join in the dancing, shall we?' she said lightly. 'That is if you've had enough to eat.'

It was well past midnight when everyone decided to leave, piling into the few cars that had brought them. As she stood in the parking-space seeing everyone off, Jilly noted that Ed's car wasn't there and wondered, as always with a twinge of jealousy, where he had gone for the evening.

'Simon doesn't have anywhere to stay for the night,' Ruth whispered in her ear. 'You have plenty of spare rooms. Why don't you let him stay here for the night or until he gets fixed up somewhere else.'

Jilly turned and caught sight of Simon. He was standing a few feet behind Ruth and looking at her in that hopeful way, as if he believed she could solve all his problems for him. Something deep inside her resented that belief of his, but she ignored it, letting her customary generosity rule her head.

'I suppose I could let him have a room here,' she said. 'But only for a short time. And I wouldn't like Irma Stratton to know. She'd probably turn me out if she thought I was providing free bed and board for island visitors.'

'It would only be for tonight and tomorrow night, wouldn't it, Simon?' said Ruth. 'Until Monday morning when everything gets going again.'

'That's right,' he said, approaching them. 'But not if it's going to cause any trouble for you, Jilly.'

'How can it cause trouble for her? We're not going to tell anyone you're staying here,' said Ruth, bossily. 'Who is to know you're here besides us?' Then she added thoughtfully, 'Except Ed Forster, perhaps. Which part of the house does he hang out in, Jilly?'

'The west wing,' said Jilly without thinking.

'And you're in the east wing and never the twain shall meet, I hope,' trilled Ruth.

'I hardly ever meet him,' said Jilly coolly, and turned to Simon. 'It won't be any trouble if you stay. You can help me clear up the mess around the pool.'

'Thanks, Jilly. You're a pal in a million,' he said softly. 'I'll just get my gear from Gerry's car.'

'Maybe he'll keep the wolf away from your door,' Ruth suggested with a touch of mockery, looking after Simon as he walked over to the other car.

'What do you mean?' asked Jilly in puzzlement. 'I'm not exactly starving right now.'

'I meant the big bad wolf called Ed Forster,' scoffed Ruth and bent to kiss Jilly's cheek. 'Nighty-night, love. See you.'

By the time Jilly, with Simon's help, had cleared away the remains of the party and she had shown him to the bedroom in the central part of the house where she thought it best for him to stay, it was almost two in the morning and she knew she should go to bed. Yet after saying goodnight to Simon, who seemed to be pretty bushed himself and in no state for an all-night session of reminiscing or exchanging confidences, she did not go to her own room. Instead she wandered out into the soft, scented darkness.

The sickle moon had gone and the stars, which always seemed bigger to her in that part of the world, glowed with golden light in the blue-black sky. Their light, coming from so far away, shimmered faintly on the sea over which she could look from the edge of the pool terrace. There was no wind and the palms were silent. It was so quiet she could hear quite clearly the sound of a car engine coming from the direction of Caracet. The car slowed down and she gripped the rail at the edge of the terrace which prevented anyone from falling down the sheer cliffs to the beach below. Excitement beat through her. Ed was coming back from wherever he had been.

She could leave the terrace, flee to her room before he appeared and avoid any confrontation with him, but she didn't. She remained where she was looking out at the starlit sea until the engine was turned off and she heard the distant slam of a door.

In rubber-soled yachting shoes his feet made no noise as he came along the path but she knew he was coming because he was whistling softly to himself. By the time he emerged from the pathway on to the terrace she was standing by the pool, ghost-like in her white dress, her pale hair picking up the faint radiance from the stars. When he saw her he stopped short.

'I thought the party would be over by now,' he said and came towards her with lazy strides. Close to her he stopped, hands on his hips. In spite of the starlight, without the floodlights on it was hard to see the expression on his face.

'It is. Why didn't you stay and join us?'

'For several reasons.' His shrug was very French. 'The

main one being I can't stand Ruth Burrows.'

'Ruth's all right. She's been a good friend to me,' she protested. 'I suppose you don't like her because she turned you down once.'

'Did she? When? Where?' She couldn't see the expression on his face but she could tell by the derisive way his voice drawled that his eyebrows would be tilted in amusement.

'I'm not really surprised you don't remember,' she retorted. 'I suppose you only remember your conquests and never your defeats.'

'So Ruth has been talking to you, has she? I thought she might. Isn't there some saying about hell knowing no fury like a woman who has been scorned? I guess she fits that description. Yet I'm glad she warned you about me.' He paused, drew a deep breath and murmured, 'Jill, about this afternoon . . .'

'Yes,' she whispered, when he hesitated, and felt her pulses leap uncontrollably.

'Try to forget it happened. It was a mistake. Mine. As usual.' His voice rasped with bitterness.

'Supposing I don't want to forget? Supposing I can't?' she cried. Emotion getting the better of her, she flung back her head to look up at him.

'You can. If you really try hard, you can. If you believe what Ruth told you, you can,' he insisted, his voice low and urgent. 'I know you're not like some of the other women, like Ruth for instance. I can guess that you're more serious, and not capable of indulging in a casual affair and ending it with no regrets.'

'You're trying to tell me you don't want me any more, aren't you?' she hissed, hurt beyond bearing because as far as she could see he was rejecting her after all. In the time he

had been away from her he had weighed her attractions for
him and had found them wanting. 'Go on, say it. Say I'm
not sexy enough, not experienced enough. I suppose you've
been with that woman in Caracet you go to see.'

'What woman in Caracet?' he said and the amused drawl
was back. She really did give him a lot to laugh at.

'The one you went to have dinner with the first night you
were here. The one you've been to see each night since you
came here. The one you stay with until the small hours.'
The words poured out of her. She sounded like some
neglected wife upbraiding her husband for infidelity, she
thought, and stopped abruptly, catching her breath.

'The woman I went to see the first night I was here was
my cousin Alicia. I had dinner with her and her husband.
You met them on the beach,' he explained coolly. 'And the
person I have been to see each night since, including
tonight, is my grandfather. He likes to play chess. But I
really don't think you have any right to question where I've
been or what I've been doing until the small hours of the
morning. Where I go and what I do is none of your damned
business.' Mortified, her cheeks burning, she nodded
miserably. 'As for not wanting you any more,' he added
more slowly, 'that isn't true either.'

It took a while for that to sink through the mortification
she was feeling for having behaved like a jealous wife, but
when it did it was as if her mind were flooded suddenly with
golden starlight.

'Then why . . .?' she began and broke off. No point in
asking a question he would either ignore or answer in some
way to put her off.

'Why do I want you to forget what happened?' he
suggested quietly. 'This is why. Probably some of what
Ruth told you about me is true too. I have a bad reputation

where women are concerned.'

'I don't care if you do,' she said, and going close to him put both her hands on his chest and slid them up over the fine cotton of his shirt. Through the material his skin seemed to burn her palms. She lifted her face to his, inhaling the fragrances of his skin and his hair. 'I like you and I want you and I wish I hadn't invited Ruth and the others to come for dinner. If they hadn't come when they did we would have been lovers by now.'

Under her hands she felt the rise and fall of his chest as he drew in a deep breath. His hands gripped her wrists as if he would have jerked her hands from him in rejection.

'You don't know what you're saying,' he whispered huskily. 'Or what you're doing.'

'Oh yes, I do. I know I'm not very experienced but I'm doing my best to induce you to make love to me again. This afternoon you made me want you and I haven't stopped wanting you since. Please, kiss me, Ed. Please.'

His hands left her wrists to hold her head, his fingers pressing hard against her temples. Down on to her mouth his lips came, hot and ruthless, ravaging the softness of her lips unmercifully. There was no sweet wooing in his kiss this time, no playful tenderness. It insulted and savaged her until she began to struggle to escape, horrified by what she had unleashed in him. At last she broke free of his hold to face him, her hair hanging dishevelled over her face, her breasts rising and falling as she gulped for breath. In his shadowed face his eyes glinted with blue fire and his teeth showed as his lips drew back from them.

'Is that what you wanted?' he challenged her jeeringly. He was short of breath too.

A hand pressed against her lips, she backed away from him and right into the swimming-pool. Arms flailing helplessly, legs in the air, she hit the water back first and sank. Displaced water surged up and covered her head, filling her ears, her eyes and her nose. She touched bottom and began to float upwards. Spluttering and coughing, half blinded, she broke surface and turning, swam to the steps at the side of the pool and clung there for a moment helplessly, still fighting for breath. From far away a voice spoke to her, a voice that drawled and was shaking with unkind laughter.

'Give me your hands. I'll help you out.'

She didn't give him her hands but he took them anyway and hauled her up the steps.

'As good a way as any of cooling your ardour,' he mocked.

'Pig. Brute,' she muttered, pulling her hands free of his. 'If you knew how much I wish you'd never survived those ocean crossings and had never come back to this island,' she seethed, and turning on her heel she walked with as much dignity as she could muster, in her soaked clinging dress and squelching sandals, into the house. He didn't follow her and didn't pretend to show concern for her half-drowned state this time, she mused bitterly when she reached her bedroom and closed the door.

In the bathroom she stripped off her wet clothes and was soon in the shower, but although the warm water was comforting, she was close to tears because Ed had treated her so roughly, as if he despised her.

In bed at last, exhausted after the most traumatic day in her life since Kevin had been killed, she crashed, falling into a deep dark pit of sleep almost as soon as she closed her eyes. For hours she slept until wakened by a continuous knocking on her bedroom door. Struggling up from the pit of oblivion she called out, 'Who's there?'

'Simon. Jilly, are you OK?'

Simon! She had forgotten all about him. Scrambling off the bed she pulled on her dressing-gown and rushed over to the door which she had locked last night. Turning the key, she opened the door. Looking both puzzled and worried, he was standing in the passage.

'What time is it?' she gasped.

'Five minutes after noon. That's why I was getting worried. Do you always sleep so late?'

'No. Not even on Sunday,' she said, rubbing her eyes. 'Thanks for waking me. Have you had breakfast?'

'I helped myself to some. The guy you were having an argument with last night by the pool came in while I was cooking it.' He looked rather embarrassed, his eyes avoiding hers.

'How do you know I was arguing with him by the pool last night?' she exclaimed.

'I heard your voices. What with the louvered windows and the shutters being wide open you can hear most of what's going on outside when you're inside the house.' A grin tugged at the corners of his mouth. 'Did he push you into the pool or did you push him into it?'

'You heard me fall into the pool?' she gasped.

'Sure did.' His grin widened. 'Must have been some argument. You and he must be very intimate to argue like that and still be friends. Who is he?'

'The brother of the woman who owns this house.'

'He told me he owns the house.'

'It isn't his house,' she retorted, 'it's Michelle's house.'

'Well, that's neither here nor there,' said Simon with a shrug. 'What's bothering me is why does he seem so familiar. Where can I have run into him?'

'In Newport, perhaps? He was there. He came in third in

the Transatlantic Race last year.'

'Then that accounts for it,' said Simon, his face clearing.
'I must have seen his picture in a yachting magazine.
Would you like me to get you some breakfast?'

'No—no, thanks. I'll get something for myself. Thanks
for waking me up.'

'Any time,' he said obligingly, his admiring glance
drifting meaningfully over her sleep-dishevelled state.

Jilly swung the door shut and leaned back against it, the
memory of the argument between herself and Ed tumbling
into her mind. How much had Simon heard? How much
had he seen? Had he seen Ed kissing her? No. Ed had more
than kissed her. He had as good as molested her, savaging
her with that ruthless kiss, treating her as if she were a
harlot.

Perhaps that was how she had seemed to him when she
had invited him to make love to her again. But she hadn't
intended to seem like that. She had been trying to show him
that she didn't care if he had a bad reputation, that she still
wanted him and could love him in spite of what other
people said about him.

It looked as if she was out of her depth this time, she
sighed, as she brushed her hair. Ed was a much more
complex personality than any other man she had known,
much more complex than Simon, for instance. She would
only have to crook her finger invitingly once to Simon and
he would come running to her. But she didn't want Simon.
He was too young and lacked the mature self-confidence
possessed by Ed Forster.

Another swift thought darted into her mind. Ed had told
Simon he owned this house. Why? She laid down the
hairbrush and stared frowningly at her own reflection. The
lilac-coloured cotton sun-top she was wearing with brief

white shorts suited her colouring. It set off the pale gold tan of her shoulders and arms and drew attention to the golden colour of her eyes. Traumatic the events of the previous day might have been, but they didn't seem to have aged her at all, she thought humorously. In fact being half drowned twice seemed to have agreed with her. Suddenly she smiled, laughing a little at herself and how she must have looked to Ed when she had gone backwards into the swimming-pool. High drama had certainly been reduced to farce. No wonder he had laughed so much.

She must see him again, perhaps to laugh with him over her dousing in the pool, to try to establish a better relationship with him and to ask him why he had told that lie to Simon about owning the house.

Leaving the bedroom, she hurried along the passage and into the kitchen. No one was there but there was evidence of people having been there. Used dishes and glasses were piled on the counter by the sink and Simon had left the milk and the bacon and butter out. Almost automatically Jilly put them away, took out the orange juice and poured some for herself and drank it. Then she went out on to the pool terrace.

Hot sunshine blazed down. The reddish tiles glowed and the pool reflected the blue sky. Yellow and purple flowers rioted with colour in the bushes. There was no wind. Noon-time was brutally bright, sizzling with heat.

Under the shade of a drooping casuarina tree on the other side of the pool she caught sight of sun-tanned legs stretched out on a lounger. Slowly she walked round the pool. Ed, not Simon, was taking his ease. He was wearing brief close-fitting swimming-shorts and a white sun-hat was tilted forward over his eyes. He looked as if he was sleeping.

'Hello,' said Jilly cheerfully. 'Have you seen Simon anywhere?'

She watched a big sun-tanned hand push the hat back a little. Within the shadow of the hat's brim his eyes were dark, looked almost black.

'Who?' he drawled.

'Simon. He said he'd been speaking to you. He said you own this house. Why did you tell him that? Why did you lie to him?'

'I didn't lie. I am part-owner of this house with Michelle. My father left it to both of us in his will. When that Simon guy wanted to know who I was and why I was staying here I told him the truth. It seemed a good way to get rid of him and it worked. He's gone.' He pulled the hat-brim down over his eyes again and lay back. 'He said to tell you he'd see you at the marina or the boatyard,' he added.

She was so astounded by what he had said, about being not only a part-owner of the house but also admitting to having wanted to be rid of Simon, that she couldn't say anything for a few seconds. His whole attitude was extremely aggravating as he lounged there ignoring her, just when she was willing to let bygones be bygones and show friendliness.

'Perhaps you would like to be rid of me, too,' she said waspishly, when she had recovered her wits.

He raised his head and gave her a long level look from under the brim of the hat.

'No, I wouldn't,' he said softly. 'But I shan't stop you if you . . .' He broke off in mid-sentence, his eyes widening as he looked past her. He swore virulently under his breath and moving with a swiftness that gave her no chance to get away grasped her nearest hand and pulled her down and across his thighs. Under her thighs she felt strong sinews flex under his hair-crisped skin as he took her weight.

'What are you doing?' she gasped, gazing up at him helplessly. She would have tried to escape, but with one big hand at her waist, his other arm sliding over her shoulders, he was bending over her in a very proprietary manner.

'We have unexpected and unwelcome visitors,' he whispered through taut lips. 'And we are about to put on a performance for their benefit.' His eyes danced suddenly with devilry and she felt the hand at her waist slide up under the edge of her sun-top. 'Do me a favour, and follow my lead in this. I'll be your friend for life, Jilly, if you do.'

'You mean . . .?'

'I mean make as if we're lovers and kiss me.'

'But why?' she was beginning, and got no further as his firm, slightly smiling lips covered hers.

It wasn't hard to do what he asked when he kissed her with such sweetness and warmth. Her lips parted willingly and her free arm went around his neck. Under her sun-top his hard fingers tensed against the soft swell of her breast and then spread out. Delicious sensations tingled through her and she stroked the back of his neck, pressing him closer to her. She felt rather than heard his soft groan of pleasure and was sinking into a mindless swirl of sensuousness when a man's voice spoke nearby.

'Looks like we've come at the wrong time, Gloria. Ed's kind of busy right now.'

CHAPTER FOUR

ED lifted his lips from hers slowly as if reluctant to withdraw. For a brief second he looked at her with sultry, heavy-lidded eyes and then turned his head from which he had swept the sun-hat when he had bent to kiss her. Still holding her close to him, his hand still cupping her breast under the brief sun-top, he looked up at the couple who were approaching them. The man was large and overweight. About sixty years of age, he had thinning brown hair and was wearing a cream-coloured shirt and baggy Bermuda shorts of bright blue. The woman was slim and elegant in a crisp linen suit. A lacy sun-hat with a broad brim was set rakishly on her shining black hair.

'I think we'll stand up to deal with this,' Ed whispered and somehow stood up, taking Jilly with him. One arm still around her, he held out his right hand to the approaching man,

'Hi, Hiram, what brings you to this island?' he said smoothly. 'On vacation?'

'No way. Would you believe I'm actually here on business?' replied the man, jovially pumping Ed's hand as if it really were a pump handle while his small bright eyes looked right at Jilly, ogling her. 'Irma Stratton told me you were in residence here and of course, as soon as she knew, Gloria wanted to come over and say hello. Irma said nothing about your having company, though.'

'This is Jill,' said Ed, easily. His arm tightened a little

about Jilly's shoulders as if in warning and he slanted a glance down at her upturned face. 'She's living here in the house right now. Meet Hiram and Gloria Presensky, from New York, Jill.'

'Pleased to meet you, Jill.' Hiram pumped her right hand in the same way as he had pumped Ed's, his loud voice overriding her softly spoken, 'How do you do?'

The woman Gloria, who had a severely classical profile, merely nodded distantly before looking up at Ed and smiling at him, showing beautiful perfectly shaped teeth.

'Ed, it's been such a long time,' she said, in a low voice. She spoke English with a slight foreign accent and Jilly wondered whether Gloria was French or Spanish or even Italian. Certainly her looks hinted at Latin blood. 'Too long,' Gloria added meaningfully, and held Ed's hand much longer than necessary.

'Guess we've come at the wrong time, though, honey,' put in Hiram. 'I warned you that people here rest after their lunch, have a *siesta* time and especially on Sunday, eh, Ed?' Hiram laughed rather coarsely and winked at Jilly. 'We'll get out of here, right now.'

'But not until we've passed on Irma's invitation to you, Ed,' Gloria interposed smoothly. 'She's having some people in for cocktails this evening and wants you to come. You will come, won't you? Both of you?' The smile Gloria gave Jilly was rather cold, a little strained. She looked so much younger than Hiram that Jilly wonderd whether she was his daughter and not his wife at all.

'What do you say, Jill?' murmured Ed, his arm squeezing her affectionately again as he half turned his head and brushed his lips against her hair. 'Are we free this evening? Would you like to go over to Irma's?'

Now did he want her to say no or yes? She gazed up at him, hoping that she was looking and behaving like one of those gormless blondes often depicted in American films and TV shows.

'I want to do whatever you want to do, honey,' she whined. 'But you know that.'

The glance he shot her was anything but amorous, she thought with an inward laugh.

'Ed, do come and afterwards we can all dine together at the Two Roses,' urged Gloria. 'Hiram has just bought the restaurant.'

'I've always wanted to have dinner there,' said Jilly, suddenly becoming herself again. 'I've heard the food is fabulous. Have you really taken it over, Hiram?'

'Sure have, honey,' said Hiram, beaming delightedly because she was taking an interest in him. 'It's a hobby of mine, looking for restaurants on these islands that need an injection of American dollars and know-how. Why don't you met us at Irma's and then go on to the opening party at the restaurant, Ed? You being a native son of the island as well as the son of a famous film actor, it would be a great bit of publicity. We're having photographs taken of all the celebrities who are to be there. And there'll be a guy there who writes up restaurants for that New York gourmet magazine.'

'Do say you'll come, Ed,' pleaded Gloria looking up at Ed as if he were some god she worshipped. Her glance, haughtily hooded by sweeping black lashes that Jilly was sure were false, swept down from the face of her idol to Jilly's face. 'I'm sure your little friend will like the food and will enjoy being among the well known people who will be there as our guests. Just think, dear,' she went on patronisingly for Jilly's benefit, 'you might get your photo in the magazine. You could arrange that, couldn't you, Hiram?'

'You betcha,' said Hiram, enthusiastically. 'You'll come even if Ed doesn't, won't you, Jill? I'll drive over personally to pick you up if he won't oblige and bring you.'

'OK, Hiram. You win.' Ed didn't sound at all enthusiastic. 'We'll meet you at Irma's and join you for dinner.'

'Great.' Hiram rubbed his podgy freckled hands together as if he were washing them. 'We'll see you later, then. Come on, Glo.' He hooked an arm through Gloria's and began to steer her away. 'Nice little place you have here, Ed,' he shouted over his shoulder. 'Built by your Dad, so I'm told, and you and that sexy sister of yours are joint owners, so Irma was saying. Yeah, it's a great piece of real estate. If you ever want to unload it, just say the word to Hiram Presensky. I know plenty who'd part with a couple of million dollars for a place like this. See you both later.'

'See you, Hiram,' drawled Ed. 'I guess that didn't go too badly,' he continued, swinging Jilly round to face him. 'But just in case Gloria didn't get the message . . .'

His hand was forceful under her chin, raising her face to the predatory swoop of his lips. Unprepared for this kiss, Jilly swayed where she stood, her hands reaching for his upper arms to hold on to. But the kiss didn't last long. He lifted his lips from hers long before her head started to whirl and long before she was able to respond.

'Good, they've gone,' he said coolly, his arms dropping to his sides. 'Thanks for helping out. But it would have been better if you hadn't said you'd always wanted to eat at the Two Roses. Now we're stuck with having to continue the performance for their benefit at Irma's happy hour and at dinner in the restaurant to say nothing of having everything made public by a photographer from a New York magazine.'

'Well, I'm so sorry,' hissed Jilly, rubbing her lips with the tips of two fingers. 'Sorry you're stuck with taking me out to dinner, I mean. How was I suppose to know you didn't want to go out with them? How was I supposed to know what the "performance" was for, come to think of it?'

His slanted grin was unrepentant as he pulled on the sun-hat again and stretched out on the lounger.

'I was hoping that when they saw how engrossed we were in each other they'd take the hint and go away. The performance was to inform Gloria, more than Hiram really, that I—to use your words of a few nights ago—am not available. She's been doing her damnedest to have an affair with me for years.'

'Why?' asked Jilly, finding that standing in the hot sun was having the effect of sapping her vitality. Or was it the effect of his kisses? She sat down on the deck-chair that was near the lounger and in the shade of the overhanging branches of the trees.

'Why what?' he growled, not looking at her, leaning against the low back of the lounger, his face half hidden by the brim of the sun-hat.

'Why has she been trying to have an affair with you?'

'Because she's like that. Hiram doesn't come up to her expectations as a husband so she's always looking round for some guy who might oblige her, flesh out her sexual fantasies for her.' His voice rasped harshly.

'And you have a reputation for doing that, I suppose,' she remarked coolly, but as soon as the words were out of her mouth she regretted them when she saw one of his hands clench into a fist. 'I'm sorry,' she apologised wholeheartedly. 'That was a nasty thing to say. And you don't have to take me to Irma's or to dinner afterwards, if you don't want to meet Hiram and Gloria again.'

He was silent for so long she wondered if he had gone to sleep and she was thinking of creeping away and into the house to have something to eat, when he sat up and swung his legs off the lounger so that he was sitting on it facing her. From under the brim of the sun-hat he stared at her steadily.

'Would you mind telling me exactly what Ruth Burrows told you about me?' he asked.

'She . . . she . . . just said you're the son of Jon Forster the movie star, and . . . and . . .' She broke off, looking away from him.

'And,' he prompted.

'That like father, like son,' she said, wishing she had managed to escape into the house.

'Meaning?'

Her glance swerved back to his face. It was hard again, the wide lips set in a stern line, the blue eyes dark, staring at her unrelentingly.

'Ed, I've told you it doesn't matter,' she began but he interrupted her again.

'Tell me what she meant by saying I'm like my father,' he ordered coldly.

'She meant that, like him, you . . . you like to play around, have affairs with lots of women.'

'You knew that about him before she told you that?' he rapped.

'No. Not really. Oh, I'd seen him in a couple of movies,

but I didn't really know anything about his private life. I'm not much interested in movie stars. I don't read articles about them and I know that a lot of the articles don't tell the truth, that they are invented for publicity purposes.'

'You can say that again,' he murmured and, resting his elbows on his knees, he leaned forward cupping his hands under his chin. 'What else did Ruth tell you?'

'That you'd . . . you'd tried it on with her, the last time you visited the island.'

'Ha.' His short laugh was mirthless. 'It was the other way round. She tried it on with me. She's like Gloria, always on the look out for a new lover. I told her to get lost. But I don't expect you to believe me. She's your friend, has been for a while, so you'll believe her rather than me.'

'But last night you said that what she had said about you was probably true,' she pointed out.

'I meant that if she had warned you that I had a reputation as a Lothario, a lover and a leaver, she was right. I do. But I hadn't realised she would bring my father into her story and lay the blame at his door for anything I do or have done, nor did I guess she would lie about her little fling with me.' He gave her an underbrowed glance, his lips twisting cynically. 'I earned my bad reputation honestly, without any help from my father. I told you he was from England, didn't I? He was born near London and trained to be an actor at the Royal Academy of Dramatic Art.'

'Yes, I knew that, read it somewhere,' she admitted,

'Like many actors he was a very shy man,' he continued musingly. 'And like many Englishmen he was also a very private person. He loathed the publicity build-up the Hollywood studio gave him as a sex symbol just because of a few hot scenes in some of his films, and he tried to get away from that sort of thing by escaping to this island and building this house. He came here to hide, to be himself, especially after his first wife left him on account of some story she heard about him having an affair with one of the women who acted opposite to him in a film. He met my mother here, fell in love with her and married her secretly. He never took her to Hollywood, but used to leave her here when he had to go and make a film. Michelle and I lived here with her when we were little kids, away from the glare of publicity. Unfortunately she died, when I was about eight. Michelle was only four. I don't think my father ever got over her death. For a while Michelle and I stayed on here with my grandfather until Dad decided that he needed us with him all the time and we moved to Los Angeles to live with him. He was a very good father, made it possible for us both to have a good education and follow careers of our own choosing. I chose naval architecture and yacht design, she chose acting, following in his footsteps.'

He paused and, taking off the sun-hat, he wiped the sweat from his brow with long fingers. Enthralled by what he was telling her, Jilly sat still, unable to take her eyes from his face.

'He died six years ago and it all came out, how he had been married to my mother secretly and how he had left this house to Michelle and me. Everyone knew at last just who we were. It was OK for Michelle. She revelled in the publicity, basked in the limelight that shone on her from being Jon Forster's daughter. It was not so good for me,' he added wryly.

'But Ruth said he was divorced from your mother.'

'She got that wrong. Probably because he married again a few years after my mother's death.' He glanced at her, a half-smile lifting a corner of his mouth. 'I've never told anyone the truth about my father before, but I want to set the record about him straight with you. I earned my bad reputation through my own irresponsible behaviour.'

'Thank you for telling me the truth about him, but you didn't need to,' she replied earnestly. 'I've tried to tell you several times that I don't care if you do have a bad reputation. I take people as I find them, make my own judgements about them.'

'I just wanted to make it clear to you that I come by my reputation honestly and owe nothing of it to my father,' he pointed out. 'And you should beware of the big bad wolf, Blondie.' He was smiling more broadly now and his eyes were beginning to dance. Leaning towards her he whispered, 'I wish I'd met you years ago.'

'How many years ago?' She didn't lean away from him.

'Fifteen.'

'Fifteen,' she repeated with a chuckle of laughter. 'I was only ten fifteen years ago. How old were you?'

'Twenty, nearly twenty-one.' His eyes had darkened again, their glance lingering on the shape of her mouth. 'Much too old for you,' he added rather sombrely.

'But not now, you're not too old for me now,' she whispered, the deckchair tipping forwards under her, and she leaned even closer to him so that there were only a few centimetres separating her lips from his.

'You're in a very precarious position in more ways than one, Mrs Carter,' he warned, his laughing breath wafting across her lips. 'Watch out.'

The warning came too late. The deckchair's front legs slid backwards and under her and she was thrown forward against him. He went back under her weight and for a few moments they lay laughing breathlessly, sprawling across the lounger, she on top of him.

'What I meant was that if I'd met someone like you fifteen years ago my life would have taken a very different course,' he murmured, holding her closely. 'We've met too late.'

'No we haven't. We've met just in time,' she argued, pushing up and a little away from him. 'I've met you just in time to reform you, to save you from becoming a middle-aged rake, like Hiram, ogling young women. And you've met me just in time to save me from becoming a frigid widowed old maid.'

'Old maids can't become widows,' he retorted, his hands curving to the shape of her breasts while his eyes smiled up into hers. 'And I don't ogle like Hiram does and I'm a good twenty-five years younger than he is.' His face sobered suddenly and his hands slid away from her. 'It's too late. You'd be better off with that young guy who was here this morning, Simon what's-his-name.'

'Then why did you get rid of him?' she demanded.

'Because I was angry with you for having dared to invite him to stay the night here. This isn't your house and Irma should have made it clear to you that you can't ask all the stray dogs you want to help over stiles to stay here,' he said curtly, shifting away from her and standing up.

'And what makes you think he'll have anything to do with me now that he knows I live in your house, considering that bad reputation of yours?' she retorted, facing him challengingly. 'Simon isn't such a stray dog as you suspect. He comes from a very good family and one day he'll inherit a fortune. His father is the owner of a chain of food stores in Britain.'

'Then I suggest you marry him and live comfortably if not happily ever after,' he snapped nastily.

He stepped away from her to the edge of the pool and dived into the water. She watched his long shape torpedo under the surface almost to the other side of the pool, near the house. He came up and reached the side of the pool with two strokes of his arms, heaved himself out and without looking back at her went into the house.

At once Jilly set off around the pool, also on her way into the house. She couldn't let him get away with a sneer like that without explaining himself. Up the steps she marched. Impossible to be cool on a day like this except under water, she thought, feeling sweat trickle down her back. Impossible to be emotionally cool too when riled by a man like Ed Forster.

She caught up with him in the kitchen. Water dripping from his still wet body, he was talking to someone on the phone, and she had to wait, seething, until he hung up. As soon as the receiver was put down on its rest she started.

'You're jealous,' she accused. 'You're jealous of Simon.'

'Now why would I be jealous of a shrimp like him?' he drawled. Hands on his hips he stood with his shapely sinewy legs apart. The wet, clinging swimming-shorts left little to the imagination and his stance, shoulders squared and head up, drew attention to all his physical attractions so much that Jilly drew in her breath sharply and looked away from him. Why, indeed, should he be jealous of Simon?

'Because I knew him before I met you. Because I invited him to stay here last night,' she replied, but her reasons sounded weak. And she was feeling weak again, too, and not only because she was hungry. She turned away from him and opened the fridge door. 'Oh, it doesn't matter,' she muttered, and began to take out bread and sliced ham for a sandwich. When she swung the door shut he had gone, presumably to his room to change. Her accusation had dripped off him much as the water from the pool had.

She was sitting at the breakfast-counter munching her much-needed sandwich when he came back through the kitchen. He was fully dressed in a navy-blue short-sleeved shirt and hip-hugging white pants. He didn't pause as he passed her but went on into the entrance hall. Almost falling in her haste to get off the stool on which she was sitting, she ran after him.

'Where are you going?' she demanded.

About to step through the open doorway he swung round slowly and looked at her with raised eyebrows.

'Why the hell should I tell you?' he drawled.

'No reason at all,' she retorted. 'I just wondered if you'd forgotten about going to Irma's for cocktails and dinner at the Two Roses.'

'No. I hadn't forgotten.' He stepped towards her, looking down at her frowningly. 'I think it would be best if we didn't go,' he said quietly. 'I don't want any photograph of us dining at Hiram's new place appearing in any magazine. And if we go we'd have to continue with the performance.' His lips quirked in a slight smile. 'And that wouldn't be wise. You've got enough to live down, now that it's known all over the island that you're sharing this house with me.'

'But if we don't turn up at Irma's Hiram will come looking for me. He said he would come and pick me up himself,' she protested, feeling disappointment surge up in her. 'And I really would like to dine at that restaurant,' she went on in an attempt to assert her own independence from him.

'So why don't you go to Irma's by yourself and then on to the restaurant with her?' he suggested reasonably.

'They'll all want to know why you're not with me,' she argued.

'Then make up some excuse.' He shrugged his shoulders as if shaking off the problem as having nothing to do with him and smiled at her. 'I'm sure something will occur to you.'

'But what about Gloria? If I turn up without you won't she guess that you and I aren't having an affair? Won't she think you're available again?'

'She might, but not if she thinks Hiram is showing too much interest in you. She's not about to lose her bread and butter to some nubile little blonde.' He grinned wickedly at her. 'Don't forget how he ogled you.'

'Oh, stop it. I think you . . . you're horrid, all of you, men I mean.'

'Good,' he said obscurely and strode out of the house.

Jilly spent the next couple of hours lying on the lounger Ed had occupied that morning and trying to read a novel about the Caribbean that she had found in the house. But after a while she gave up reading, deciding that the situation in which she had landed as a result of living in a house half owned by a man like Ed was far more interesting and involved than the plot of the novel.

Leaving the lounger, she wandered back into the house and through the living-rooms, observing them closely for the first time since she had moved in. Elegant and spacious yet completely contemporary in furnishings and design, the rooms were entirely impersonal, she thought. There

were no photographs on the walls of anyone who had lived
in the house. None at all of its original owner, the actor Jon
Forster. Sinking down on one of the cream-coloured
chesterfields in the big salon, she looked out of the wide
picture windows at the view from the back of the house, at
the hills beyond the lagoon that seemed like shapes cut out
of emerald green paper by a child and stuck on the brilliant
blue of the sky.

Leaning back, she tried to remember what Jon Forster
had looked like and finally recalled a chiselled elegant
profile under a drooping wave of fair hair. Ed wasn't like
his father in looks. Not only was his hair black but his
features were more roughly hewn, more like his French
grandfather's, and physically he was much bigger than Jon
Forster had been. Only his eyes were similar, that intense,
almost fiery blue. Michelle was the one who had inherited
the fine features that photographed so well although she
was dark-haired too, and had large brown bedroom eyes.
Michelle had also inherited the shyness and the ability to
act.

Not that Ed was bad at acting, she thought, scowling
sourly, thinking of the way he had kissed her and had
behaved in front of Hiram and Gloria.

It had been a performance, put on especially for Gloria
and nothing else. But how she wished it had been for real.
Closing her eyes, she relived those moments when she had
lain across Ed's thighs and he had kissed her, trying to lose
herself in a dangerous fantasy, ignoring his warnings about
himself.

The shrilling of the telephone bell jolted her out of the
sensuous daydream. Jumping to her feet, she ran out into

the kitchen wishing there was more than one phone in the house.

'Jilly, that you? Simon, here. Phoned earlier but there was no answer.'

'I must have been outside. Where are you?'

'Down at the marina. Listen, I've been invited to have dinner at some sort of shindig in Caracet, at the opening of a restaurant by its new owner. The Two Roses. Ever heard of it?'

'I have. Who invited you?'

'Your boss, Piet Block. Seems I can take a partner with me and it was suggested to me that you might like to come.'

'Who suggested it to you. Piet?'

'Yes. Would you like to go?'

'Yes, I would, please.' It would be better than waiting for Hiram to call for her, better than having to make excuses to him and Gloria for Ed's absence, better to be seen with Simon than with Ed. 'Where shall we meet?'

'I'm going over with the Blocks so could you drive over there by yourself? We'll meet you in the bar at about seven.'

'I'll be there. Thanks, Simon.'

'You're welcome,' he replied politely and hung up. He hadn't sounded particularly friendly, she mused, as she went to her bedroom to choose a dress to wear later. Perhaps he was still miffed at being told to leave the house by Ed. Oh, well, that had been her fault. She should never have let herself be persuaded by Ruth to let Simon stay the night. But then Irma Stratton might have let her know that Ed was a joint owner of the house with Michelle, she argued. If she had the opportunity tonight she would have a word with Irma about that. Call me if you have any problems, Irma had said. Well, she had a problem, a big one. She had fallen in love with a man who didn't believe in love, who at some time in his past life had had his feelings severely hurt. By a woman, of course. And ever since then he had avoided falling in love, taking his revenge by making a certain type of woman fall in love with him.

It was just her luck to fall for someone like that, she thought morosely. After spending nearly a whole year in a deep-freeze condition after Kevin's death she had to meet and fall in love with a predator like Ed. She must be nuts.

Perhaps it wouldn't last long, this state of infatuation. Perhaps it would fade as soon as Ed moved out of the house and sailed away from the island. She hoped that would be soon. If he didn't leave soon she would have to move out of this house herself. Perhaps that was what she should do, move out. She would ask Irma tonight.

The dress she chose to wear, made from pale green sea-island cotton printed all over with a design of palm fronds, was rather crushed, so she spent a while ironing it in the kitchen. Then she took a bath, and spent some time on her hair and her fingernails. Outside the sun set in its usual blaze of glory and by the time she walked down to her car night had fallen. The moon was climbing up above the mountains and the stars were beginning to glow.

She parked in the car park by the market stalls that faced the harbour in Caracet, not far from the restaurant. On the dark grey water yachts nodded at anchor, their riding-lights swinging like displaced glow-worms high above their decks. There were an abnormal number of cars in the park for a Sunday evening in the charming little French town and the pavement in front of the restaurant was thronged with people, mostly Americans.

She entered the bar by the entrance from the main street of the town rather than by another door opening on to the market place, from which a staircase led up to the restaurant on the second floor. Simon was watching for her and came to greet her. He had tidied himself up and looked fairly spruce in a white shirt and grey trousers.

'You look great, Jilly,' he said as if he was determined now to be friendly. 'Come over here.'

Taking her hand, he led her between small round tables, where groups of people sat drinking and chattering, to a table in a corner where Piet and Marcha were sitting with Irma. As soon as she saw Jilly, Irma, who was swathed in a flowing voile caftan and had a turban of the same material wound around her head, stood up. Many bangles clashed on her long thin arms and long ear-rings touched her shoulders but her smile at Jilly was, as always, kindly yet shrewd, her grey eyes almost disappearing in the network of wrinkles around them.

'Nice to see you, Jilly,' she murmured. 'When Ed called in to see me this afternoon to tell me he couldn't come to my party or to dinner here, he was most concerned that I should find some way to get you here, to dinner, without Hiram coming to pick you up. I immediately thought of Piet and Marcha and suggested to Ed he ask them to bring you and now here you are. Much better for you to be seen here with your friend Simon than with either Ed or Hiram, I think. Now just relax and enjoy yourself. See you all later.'

'Wait, Irma, please.' Jilly stepped after the older woman who turned, frowning rather irritably.

'Now what is it?' she snapped.

'What about Gloria Presensky?' Jilly asked, aware that

Simon could be listening, as well as the people at the next table.

'What about Gloria? Jilly, couldn't it wait? I have guests with me. We'll have lunch together tomorrow, I'll call you at the boatyard to set a time and place.' Irma didn't conceal her impatience.

'What will she think when she sees me here without Ed?' persisted Jilly.

'God knows. And does it matter? You mustn't worry about Gloria. Besides, anyone has only to take one look at you to see you're just not Ed's type. See you tomorrow for lunch.'

Irma wafted away between the tables and with a sigh of frustration Jilly sat down in the chair Simon held out for her, and for the next couple of hours tried her best to enjoy herself as Irma had instructed her.

CHAPTER FIVE

THE pinging of the alarm clock penetrated the dream Jilly was having and she reluctantly opened her eyes. She had been dreaming that she and Ed were getting married. They had been standing side by side in front of the vicar of the old Norman church in the village where her parents lived in England and as the vicar had said, 'You may now kiss the bride,' the dratted alarm had gone off.

She reached out and stopped the pinging and lay back against the pillow again. Monday morning and she had a hangover, no doubt about that. Too much fine French cooking and too much wine. The Two Roses restaurant had really lived up to its reputation for fabulous food. Everything had been perfect and the wine had been so smooth she had hardly noticed she had been drinking it. That was why she had drunk too much, she supposed.

Although Jilly was sure they had both seen her, Gloria and Hiram had ignored her. Since she hadn't been accompanied by Edouard Forster she hadn't been worthy of their attention, she suspected. No point in taking her photograph while she was dining in Hiram's latest acquisition. She was a nobody and had been accompanied by nobodies, in Gloria's and Hiram's estimation.

Simon had been very sweet to her and after dinner she had walked with him along the quayside, below the high headland of rock on which the walls of the old French fort of Caracet stood, its grey flinty stones occasionally glinting in the moonlight. Together they had stood and had watched the surge of water against the rocks. They had

81

looked out across the dark moon-shimmered sea to the distant lights of the island of Angosta, had listened to the sigh of waves and the rustle of palm fronds.

They had reminded each other about the crossing of the Atlantic they had both made in Reg Turner's yacht and, when they had run out of shared memories, Simon had told her of the delights of cruising on windjammers among the islands of the State of Maine and some of the highlights of his voyage south in the autumn to the Virgin Islands.

'But all the time I was thinking about you, wishing you had been with me,' he had said. 'Looking forward to the time when I could see you again, hoping that when I did you'd have got over Kevin's death. You have, haven't you?'

'I think so. Or at least I've come to terms with it. I know now that a part of me died when he died. Or perhaps I should put it this way. A part of my life came to an end. With Kevin's accident my youth came to an end. Now I'm all adult, not a different person, but older, and ready to start building a new life for myself.'

'I'm glad to hear it,' he had replied and had slipped an arm about her waist. 'Jilly, I owe you an apology, for the way I rushed off this morning without saying anything,' he continued. 'The truth of the matter is that when Ed Forster told me he was living in the house while you're living there too, something seemed to explode in my head. I went a little crazy with jealousy, I suppose. I'd come all that way south just to see you, only to find you living in the same house as a strange man. You can guess what I thought. I hope you'll forgive me for believing the worst. Please show me that you do.'

At that point his arm had tightened about her and before she had been able to fend him off he had kissed her. She had let him in order to find out how she would respond, but the touch of his lips had lit no fire within her as the touch of

Ed's lips had done and she had felt no desire to hold him close, to stroke his hair or part her lips beneath his. Even when the pressure of his mouth against hers had increased nothing much had happened until she had felt the sickness of revulsion rising within her and, suddenly disliking the moist heat of his lips which had seemed to slobber over hers, she had laid her hands against his chest and, wrenching her mouth from his, she had pushed him away from her.

'Jilly,' he had breathed, stepping after her, arms reaching towards her. 'Now I know I was wrong and that there's nothing between you and Forster.'

'How do you know that? Who told you that there's nothing between him and me?' she had demanded, stepping back from him again.

'Forster did, not in as many words, but he implied that you and he aren't intimately involved. He was at the marina this afternoon. He'd come there to meet Piet Block who had been out sailing. He introduced me to Piet and then he suggested Piet invite me to dinner at the Two Roses and that it might be a good idea if I gave you a call and asked you to go to the dinner too.' Simon had paused then had added, 'Before he left he said he realised what I must be thinking about you living in the same house as him and that I'd jumped to the wrong conclusion. That was when he said there's nothing between you and him.'

'He lied to you,' Jilly had said through gritted teeth. 'He lied when he said there's nothing between us.'

'You mean you are having an affair with him?'

'Yes, I do. Oh, we haven't been to bed together. Not yet,' she had said forcefully and she had been secretly surprised by her own recklessness. 'But we are having an affair. A torrid tropical affair.' Inside she had been seething with irritation caused by Ed's arrogant assumption that he could organise her life for her by arranging for Simon to take her out to dinner.

By the light shed from one of the quayside lamps Simon's face had looked so mystified that she could have burst out laughing if she hadn't been so furious with Ed.

'But I don't understand,' he had bleated. 'Why would he say he isn't amorously involved with you if he is? Why would he lie about it?'

'He's trying to protect his reputation. It wouldn't do for anyone on the island to believe he's involved with anyone as ordinary as I am,' she had replied a little wildly as she had remembered Irma's remark in the restaurant bar about her not being Ed's type. 'I mean you can't keep up a reputation as a great lover unless you're seen around with the right sort of woman, you know, with the wives of wealthy men or with film actresses who have already been married several times. That's how you build up a reputation. Living in the same house as a nondescript sailmaker does nothing to add to your glamour.'

'I don't know what you're talking about, Jilly,' Simon had interrupted her tirade. 'But it seems to me you've drunk too much wine. And I have to disagree with you. You're not ordinary or nondescript. You never have been and you never will be. Even when you were married to Kevin I felt attracted to you but I'm more so now, since I've met you again.' He had grasped both her hands and had tried to pull her towards him. 'Jilly,' he had whispered. 'Jilly, I want you and I'd like to marry you. Will you come back to England with me? My old man is pestering me to go back and join the business. He says I've done enough wandering around. Jilly, say yes, and come with me. I'm going to help Gerry and Sue sail their yacht back to Britain by way of Bermuda. They say they're willing to have you as an extra crew too.'

She had to admit she had been surprised by his proposal.

She had stood and stared at him in amazement, her hands limp in his, and a cynical little thought had crept into her mind. Strange how attractive she seemed to be to men she didn't want, to Hiram and now to Simon. Why? Was it because both of them believed she was available because they believed her to be involved with Ed?

'No,' she had said loudly and clearly, taking her hands out of Simon's. 'I don't want to go back to England right now. I'm having too good a time here. And I don't want to be married again. Not yet. I've just come alive again, come out of the deep freeze of widowhood.'

'Then forget the marriage bit and just come with me on Sue's and Gerry's boat,' Simon had urged. 'We can talk about marriage when we get to England and . . .'

'You're asking me to be your lover?' she had demanded, her voice rising shrilly as she had taken offence at his assumption that she would be so obliging as to share his bed.

'Yes, I am,' he had replied. 'It isn't as if you're a virgin and would want to be married first. I mean having been married once you have some experience and . . .'

'No, Simon, the answer is no again. I don't want you as a lover or a husband.'

'But, Jilly,' he had begun and had reached out to her.

'No, no, no.' She had dodged around him and had run along the quay towards the car park. He had caught up with her as she had been unlocking the door of her car.

'I'm not driving you back to the marina,' she had declared. 'You can get a taxi. Over there.' She had waved a hand in the direction of the taxi-stand on the other side of the street and had slid into the driver's seat, slamming the door so that she couldn't hear him say 'Jilly' again.

She had driven back to the House of Doves slowly. The grey car had been in the parking-space but the only light on in the house had been in the entrance hall. If there had been a light shining out of the window of Ed's bedroom she would have gone in and asked him why he had gone to such trouble to ensure that she had been invited to dinner at the Two Roses by Simon. But the light had been off so she had gone to bed herself.

And now it was another day and time she got up to go to work. Groaning, she slid off the bed and went through the usual routine, first to the kitchen to start the coffee, back to the shower to wake herself up properly, back to the kitchen, fully dressed, for coffee and toast, then out to the car to find Ed had beaten her to it and had already left.

He was there in the boatyard, already at work on the hulls of his trimaran when she drove in through the gate and parked. But although he must have known she had arrived he didn't call a greeting to her nor she to him. In the office Piet teased her as he always did about being late and Marcha offered her some aspirin for her headache. Piet followed her up to the sail-loft and soon she was engrossed in looking at the designs he had brought for some sails that had been ordered by one of the visiting yachtsmen.

Irma called as she had said she would and arrangements were made for Jilly to meet her for lunch at an Italian restaurant on Front Street. Promptly at one o'clock Jilly descended from the sail-loft, glad to escape from the heat up there, and went out into the sunny, windy day. She walked to Front Street by way of the beach, hoping to clear away the last vestiges of her headache.

'So what did you think of dinner last night?' said Irma. Lean and angular in pink slacks and a loose white shirt, she still jangled with bracelets as she put her elbows on the table and supported her long chin on linked fingers. Her fine fair hair was swept up into a knot on top of her head.

'It was very good,' said Jilly, studying the menu. Although her head had ceased to ache, her stomach was revolting at the thought of more food. 'I think I'll just have a Caesar salad,' she said.

'It was sweet of Ed to arrange for you to come with young Simon,' drawled Irma as she studied the menu. 'Instead of coming with him, I mean. Certainly put paid to Gloria's suggestion that you and Ed were having an affair. I think I'll have a salad too. Must watch the old figure, you know, after a blow-out like last night.' The waiter came and they gave their orders. He went away.

'Gloria was only suggesting what she believed to be true,' said Jilly. 'When she was at the house Ed went to a lot of trouble to convince her that he and I were having an affair. To keep her off his back, he said. So I can't understand why he arranged for me to go to the dinner with Simon.'

'Told me he didn't want that creep Hiram turning up at the house and picking you up to take you to the dinner. He told me, too, about the little performance you helped him put on for Gloria's benefit.' Irma's thin painted lips twitched slightly. 'Very wicked of him, but I can fully understand why he doesn't want to get entangled with her. He can relax now, though. She and Hiram flew out of here this morning, down to Aruba to look at another of Hiram's investments. And I want you to know, Jilly, that I would never have suggested you look after the house for Michelle if I'd known Ed was coming here. I didn't have anywhere else for you to move into when he turned up but I have now. A house near the airport. It belongs to a Canadian couple. She's pregnant and doesn't feel too well so they've decided to abandon their usual stay of three months and return to Toronto so that she can see her own doctor. They would like someone to live in the house. You could have it until next November.'

'Why don't they rent it out, to tourists?' asked Jilly.

'They would prefer the same person to live in it for the

next ten months rather than be bothered with changeovers. They also want someone who'd be prepared to do some work in the house. They're willing to let you have it rent-free if you'd do some upholstery work for them. I think it would be the answer to your dilemma.'

'What dilemma?' asked Jilly, being deliberately obtuse.

'There would be no more talk about you and Ed living together if you move out of his house,' said Irma flatly. 'It seems he's going to be around much longer than I had thought at first. He invested money in the boatyard last time he was here and now he's thinking of staying around to design and build some yachts here on the island. Naturally he'll be wanting to live in his own house.'

The waiter came with their salads, a basket of fresh Italian bread and dishes of butter as well as two cups of coffee. Jilly looked out of the wide window beside her at the green and glinting bay. The schooner on which Simon had come from the Virgin Islands and before that from Maine was hoisting sail, the white dacron shimmering in the sunlight as it billowed out. Beyond the entrance of the harbour, an island, a sheer-sided pointed mountain of violet-grey rock, seemed to float on the gold-flecked aquamarine sea.

'So when would you like to meet the Leonards, the couple from Canada?' asked Irma, with her real-estate agent's persistence. 'They are willing to take my word that you're OK but I'd prefer it if they met you and interviewed you first.'

Jilly pushed at her salad with a fork. Had Ed hinted to Irma that he would like her to move out? It was possible, she supposed. Yet when she had asked him yesterday if he wanted her to leave he had said that he didn't. He had been going to say more but had been interrupted by the arrival of Gloria and Hiram. 'I don't want to move out. I love the house and I really don't mind sharing it,' she said.

'I understand how you feel and I was sure it would work out. In fact it did seem to be working out. If only that awful Gloria hadn't turned up. Of course I know he does have a bad reputation but . . .'

'Or so he would have us all believe,' said Jilly.

'Oh, it's true. Don't doubt it,' said Irma. 'Michelle despairs of him. She's told me so. And it's always been with another man's wife that he's become involved.'

'Women like Gloria who, when their husbands don't come up to their expectations, look around for a man who can flesh out their sexual fantasies, I suppose.'

'Mmm. Something like that.' Irma gave her a surprised glance. 'That was very well said,' she remarked. 'All your own work?'

'No, someone else said it.'

'Somehow I didn't think you'd make such a cynical observation about your own sex,' said Irma, her eyes bright and quizzical.

'Ed made the observation yesterday when he was talking about Gloria,' admitted Jilly. 'You wouldn't know anything that might have happened to Ed, fifteen years ago, would you?'

'No.' Irma shook her head. 'I've only been on the island five years and I know very little about him and Michelle apart from the fact that Jon Forster was their father. What sort of thing do you mean?'

'Something that might have hurt his feelings and made him cynical about women.'

'Mmm. I see what you mean. An unhappy love affair at the age of twenty or twenty-one could have a devastating effect on a young man. I know that because I have two sons myself. Very touchy at that age, they are. You couldn't give me any leads, could you?'

'He did say that he once eloped with a married woman and it caused a scandal. And another time he said he once did something that made a lot of people he cared for extremely unhappy.'

'Sounds absolutely fascinating.' Irma's eyes opened wide and began to twinkle. 'And just the sort of thing to dangle in front of a romantic soft-hearted young widow like you.'

'What are you getting at?' Jilly asked uneasily.

'This is a very experienced, sophisticated man you're dealing with, my dear, never doubt it. He knows just what bait to use and how to dangle it when he's fishing the stream, when he's looking around for a new lover. And he's hooked you well and truly. You believe him and you're about to fall head over heels in love with him,' remarked Irma shrewdly.

'He hasn't hooked me,' said Jilly hotly. 'Are you trying to tell me that he made up that story about having eloped with a married woman and having made people he cared for extremely unhappy?'

'I'm trying to point out to you that it's often a trick men will use to impress a woman like you. He's playing for your sympathy. Once you're sympathetic towards him he knows the rest will follow automatically. You've already tried to excuse his cynicism to me by suggesting it must have been caused by some unhappy affair. The sooner you move out of that house the better for you, before you're really hooked and landed. I'll expect you at my office around five-thirty when you've finished work. To meet the Leonards.' Irma's grey eyes were both stern and sad. 'It's for your own good, Jilly. I feel very responsible for getting you into this situation and I'd like to get you out of it before you're badly hurt.'

'All right. I suppose you're right. I should move out,' Jilly sighed unhappily. 'I'll see you at five-thirty.'

She was glad she had plenty of work to do for the rest of the afternoon. It saved her from dwelling on her dilemma, as Irma had called it. She supposed she had been letting her romanticism run away with her, romanticising Ed, even though he had warned her not to. It would be best if she moved out of his house. She could see him most days at the boatyard if she wanted to.

When she left the sail-loft at five she waited in the office for Marcha to finish speaking on the phone because she wanted to leave a message for Piet. As she lingered by the window that looked out on to the harbour where the moored yachts were silhouetted against the bright glare of the sun as it was sinking towards the horizon, she couldn't help listening to what Marcha was saying.

'He is not here right now, *madame.* Of course I will give him the message. You will be arriving on Saturday afternoon on a flight from Miami and you would like him to meet you. Would you like him to call you back? No? OK. Just pass on the message. I'll do that. Goodbye.'

Marcha put down the receiver and groaned. 'What a woman. One of Ed's French friends. Coming to visit him.' She wrote something on a pad of paper, tore off the note, folded it and handed it across the desk to Jilly. 'You'll see him before I will because I won't be here tomorrow morning. The dentist is in town and I need his attentions very badly. Don't forget now, Jilly, to pass on that message or he'll have one very angry lady on his hand. She's expecting to stay at the House of Doves.'

'Who is she? Do you know?'

'His latest girlfriend, I expect,' said Marcha carelessly. 'Now what was it you wanted me to tell Piet?'

In the pure golden light of the last hour of daylight Jilly drove to Caracet along the main route linking the Dutch port with the French one. It was always easy to tell when one had passed from Dutch territory into French without looking at the small sign beside the road that indicated you were now in the Republic of France. The surface of the road improved dramatically as you passed from Dutch soil to French. Otherwise the landscape was just the same rolling fields, rising up to the green pointed hills, crossed by the occasional dry-stone walls built by the early French settlers who had come mostly from Brittany and Normandy.

Soon she was turning into the main street of Caracet, driving down its slope towards the quayside, passing pastel-coloured French colonial buildings with second-floor balconies and shuttered windows. Many of the ground floors of the buildings, the original basements and storage areas, were now restaurants and boutiques, the shops selling everything from T-shirts and postcards to fine imported porcelain and silver and gold jewellery.

She turned off the main street before she reached the harbour and drove along the Rue de la Liberté, past the school, the police station and the bakery, until she came to a narrow alleyway shaded by lush shrubs and trees. After parking the car at the side of the street she walked down the alley to a group of old renovated buildings that overlooked the harbour where Irma had her simple two-roomed office.

Two hours later when the velvet darkness of the tropical night had engulfed everything and lights were twinkling from houses, she drove back to the House of Doves from the house owned by the couple from Canada. The young couple had been very pleasant and most eager to have her live in their house for some months as long as she would make new curtains for the windows, re-upholster their furniture and supervise the laying of new carpets. The house itself was comfortable enough and was near a pretty beach and one of the big resort hotels. She had told them she would think about it and would let them know as soon as possible. They would be leaving the island on Saturday.

It all depended on how Ed reacted to her leaving. She guessed he would probably be relieved to know she had found somewhere else to live. In fact she wouldn't be at all surprised if he wasn't in a conspiracy with Irma to get her to move out because he was expecting a visitor from France.

His car was in the parking-space and lights seemed to be blazing out from every window of the house. The pool terrace was dappled with the moving shadows of leaves. A light breeze sang a song in the trees and far below on the beach the waves whispered.

She would miss this house when she moved, Jilly thought with a sigh as she entered it. During the month she had stayed in it she had developed an affection for it. And also for its joint owner . . . Her thoughts swerved away from that suggestion and she busied herself getting something to eat. No point in getting sentimental about a house. Or about a man. She had known when she had come to live there she would have to leave it eventually and leaving it didn't mean she wouldn't ever see Ed again. She would see him every day at the boatyard while he was working there. Unless he made it difficult for her to stay there too. As Piet's business partner he probably had a say in the hiring and firing of workers.

After eating she rinsed through the dishes she and Ed had used and put them in the dishwasher. It didn't contain enough dirty things for her to go to the expense of using gallons of water so she would wait until they had used more dishes. She switched off lights in the kitchen, breakfast-room and dining-room, and leaving one table-lamp lit in the living-room she stepped out through one of the sliding glass patio windows on to the deck that ran the full width of the back of the house.

She was leaning on the rail looking out at the glimmer of water in the lagoon and the dark hills beyond it, admiring the pale golden sheen of the newly risen moon when a crash from inside the house startled her. Whirling round she ran through the living-room and into the kitchen, her hand going to the switch on the wall. Light flooded the room. Ed was sitting on the floor examining the tipped-over counter stool into which he must have walked.

'What happened?' Jilly asked, although she could guess.

'What do you think happened?' he snarled at her. 'I tripped over the bloody stool. Could have maimed myself for life. Why the hell do you have to switch off all the lights?'

'Because I was brought up to use electricity economically,' she retorted. 'Why do you have them all on?'

'Because I like to see where I'm going,' he snapped, getting to his feet and limping across to another stool. He leaned against it, rubbing one of his knees.

'Well, you could have switched on the lights in here as you came into the room,' she pointed out, wondering if he had really hurt himself. Recalling what Irma Stratton had told her about the possibility of his making up stories about himself in order to gain her sympathy she was suddenly very wary of him. Pretending to be badly hurt was another male trick to get attention, she recalled. 'There is a switch on the wall just inside the door as you enter from the west wing,' she added coolly.

He gave her a cold scathing glance and continued to rub his knee but decided to make no comment.

'When did you get in?' he asked truculently.

'Oh, about half an hour ago,' she replied lightly. 'Marcha asked me to give you this.' She took the folded note of paper from her skirt pocket and handed it to him. As he took the note from her his long fingers grasped hers and prevented her from moving away. Under black eyebrows his eyes were blue-black, as dark as the storm-clouds that sometimes built up in the sky at the end of a hot day.

'Why have you taken so long to come back here? Where have you been until now?' he demanded gruffly.

'Why the hell should I tell you?' she retorted, mimicking the tone of voice he had used to her the previous afternoon, and turning away, she walked out of the kitchen.

In the living-room she squatted before the collection of records which were stacked under the record-player. She selected one of her favourites, a guitar concerto by the Spanish composer Rodrigo, and, standing up again, opened the turntable to put it on. When the room was filled with the sound of richly exotic melodies played by a symphony orchestra she took some writing-paper and an envelope from the small writing-desk. Sitting down on one of the luxurious deep-seated and cushioned chesterfields, she began to write a letter to her parents, resting the paper on a book she took from a coffee-table.

The music turned up loud weaved about her, insulating her against any other sound in the house. The second movement, often intensely romantic in atmosphere, was in full swing and she was on the second sheet of notepaper, writing carefully so that her handwriting would be understood as she described her outing to the Two Roses restaurant the night before, and listed some of the celebrities she had spotted dining there for her parents' interest, when the volume of the music was suddenly reduced. She looked up sharply. Ed was standing just in front of the stereo, regarding her from under frowning eyebrows.

'Do you have to have it turned up so loudly?' he complained. 'It's a wonder you're not deaf.'

'To get the full effect of the orchestration in the stereophonic sound the volume should be turned up,' she retorted coolly, looking down at her letter pointedly. 'If you don't like the music you could always go to another part of the house where you wouldn't be able to hear it.'

'Perhaps this is where I should remind you that this house is mine and I can turn down the stereo if I want to. If you want to listen to loud music get yourself some ear-phones, then you won't trouble anyone else,' he growled.

'My, my, you are grouchy, aren't you?' she remarked. 'Never mind, after this week you won't have to worry about having me around. I'm moving out on Saturday.'

'Where are you going?' he said sharply, as if he cared.

'I thought we'd more or less decided that is a question neither of us should ask the other and that neither of us should answer,' she retorted sweetly, and started to write again, her head bent so that she couldn't see him.

She didn't hear him move, only knew that he had when the cushions beside her sank beneath his weight. The warmth of his body radiated out to her and the scents of his skin and hair swirled about her. Her hand shook and she was forced to stop writing. If she had continued no one would have been able to make sense of what she had written because it wouldn't have made sense. Pen poised just above the paper she waited tensely for his next move.

First he took the pen from her fingers and laid it down on the coffee-table. Then he picked up the book with the sheets of notepaper and put them down beside the pen. Folding her hands together so that he wouldn't notice them shaking she laid them on her lap and stared at them.

'There is something I'd like to clear up, a question I have to put to you which I hope you can answer,' he said with a sort of silky menacing note in his voice. 'There's a rumour going about that you and I are having an affair. The exact words, as quoted to me were, "a torrid tropical affair". Any comment?'

Wholly shaken by what he had just said, she raised her head and looked at him. He was very close. His eyes, still a dark stormy blue, were on a level with hers.

'Who . . . who . . .?' Her lips were dry and she had to lick them before she could go on. 'Who told you that?' she croaked.

'Never mind who told me. It's the subject of gossip tonight throughout the yachting community of the island and my guess is that it's giving some people a hell of a good laugh. Did you or did you not tell someone we're having an affair?'

'I . . . er, yes, I did.' She glanced away from his eyes which were looking so accusingly into hers. 'I told Simon. But he had no right to go around telling other people what I told him in a purely private and personal conversation,' she said defensively.

'Why did you tell him that?' he demanded, still menacingly.

'For the same reason you asked me to put on that performance for Gloria's benefit,' she replied. 'He was being a nuisance.'

'In what way?'

'Oh, kissing me and wanting me to go with him back to England, wanting me to be his lover.'

'That was the only reason?' he persisted. Some of the storminess had faded from his eyes. They were beginning to sparkle again and a slight smile tugged at the corners of his lips.

'No, it wasn't,' she admitted slowly. 'I also said it because I wanted to get my own back on you for making a date for me with him, arranging for him to ask me to go out to dinner with him. You had no right to do that.'

'But I thought you'd always wanted to go to dinner at the Two Roses. And it was much better for you to be seen with him than with me. Or with Hiram,' he drawled. He turned and laid his head against the back of the chesterfield, stretching his legs out before him. 'I thought I was doing you a good turn.'

'You don't seem to be getting the point I'm trying to make,' she said with a touch of impatience. 'I did want to go to dinner at the Two Roses, but I object to your thinking you can organise my life for me. You wouldn't like it if I did the same for you. You don't like anyone asking you where you're going or where you've been. You like to think of yourself as a free spirit. Well, the same goes for me. And now, if you don't mind, I'd like to finish my letter.'

'Couldn't you have thought of something better to deter friend Simon from kissing you and importuning you?' he asked, and now there was a definite undercurrent of amusement in his voice. 'Something a little less blatantly suggestive than a torrid tropical affair. It's going to take some living down.' His shoulders shook with silent laughter.

'It won't be difficult to live down once it's known I'm not living in your house any more. Something else will come up for them all to gossip about and our affair will be forgotten,' she said with a cold practicality she wasn't feeling. He sat up again, turning to face her.

'Without our ever having had the affair,' he remarked wryly, the laughter dying in his eyes and being replaced by the stormy expression again. 'That's what is going to be so hard to take,' he said, his voice softening and deepening as he leaned towards her. 'It's been good having you around, Blondie, even if you have been a little irritating at times. I'm going to miss you.'

'If I'm irritating you are ... you are ...' she began but couldn't go on because her bones were melting and her breath was catching in her throat. For some reason she couldn't move away from him, couldn't look away from him.

'I'm what?' he murmured, his lips very close to hers.

'Extremely aggravating,' she mumbled.

Somehow she managed to slide sideways and off the chesterfield before he could kiss her. 'I'll finish this letter in my room,' she gasped and, snatching the notepaper and her pen from the coffee-table, she ran from the room and along the passage to her bedroom. Once inside, she slammed the door and leaned against it panting, her head tipped back, her eyes closed as she struggled to suppress the desires that were surging up within her just because Ed had sat too close to her and had nearly kissed her, wondering what she would do if he followed her and continued to excite her emotions until she didn't care what he did to her or how she responded.

He didn't follow her and after a while her heart stopped pounding, the fires of desire died down within her and she was able to finish writing her letter, filling up the pages with a description of the Leonards' house, the date of when she would be moving into it and how long she expected to stay in it. She said nothing to her parents as to why she was leaving the House of Doves.

She spent another wretched almost sleepless night thinking about Ed and wishing she hadn't committed herself to moving out then, contrarily, wishing that she could move out before Saturday. If she could move out tomorrow it would be over and done with. As it was the next few days and nights were going to be difficult to get through as she did her best to avoid him both at work and at the house.

Next morning she felt jaded and looked it, she thought ruefully. There were dark lines scored under her eyes and the corners of her mouth drooped. If she wasn't careful her hair would start going grey, she admonished herself with a grin, as she went through to the kitchen. And it didn't help to see Ed there, looking rested and full of vitality, his tanned skin glowing with health, his black hair twisting and coiling attractively about his brow and ears as it dried.

So affected was she by his presence in the kitchen that she left the house without breakfast, vowing to keep clear of him even if it meant getting up earlier to leave the house before he was up and not returning in the evening until she was sure he had gone out again or was in bed.

At work that day it wasn't hard to avoid him because he didn't come into the office or the sail-loft. She was just leaving at five o'clock wondering how best to put in the time for the next few hours when she saw Ruth striding towards her.

'Hi. Thought you might like to come over to the marina bar and have a drink. Raoul has gone off to some meeting of skippers and so I have a free evening. We could have a bite to eat too, if you like. Unless of course you have to rush off to be with your torrid tropical lover.' Ruth's grin was taunting.

'I don't have to rush off anywhere,' said Jilly coolly. 'I'd like to have a drink with you and supper too. And where did you get the idea that I have a lover?'

They began to walk through the boatyard ducking under the bows of hauled-out boats and avoiding potholes.

'From Simon Travis. He was going on about you last night, at the marina. He'd had too much to drink and was really nasty. He kept on saying how mistaken he had been about you. How he had believed you were chaste and wholesome and all that rot, and how he'd found out you're having a torrid tropical affair with a rotter, and that you didn't care who knew it. I tell you, Jilly, he was really offensive. He only shut up when someone pointed out to him that Ed had come into the bar. It's not true, is it, what he was saying?'

'No, it isn't true,' sighed Jilly as they went through the boatyard gateway and out on to the narrow roadway, turning right to walk to the marina. The evening was calm, and the water in the bay was tinted crimson from the sunset glow. The tide was ebbing and yachts were slowly swinging round to point their bows towards the head of the harbour where lights were beginning to glitter from the windows of buildings. 'And you'll be glad to know, I'm sure,' she added, 'that I'm moving out of the House of Doves on Saturday. Irma has found me other accommodation.'

'That's great,' said Ruth enthusiastically. 'I knew you'd see sense and get out. And that piece of news should stop all the gossip. Pity you can't move out sooner.'

'Yes, it is,' agreed Jilly. 'But the Leonards aren't leaving until Friday. Anyway, I don't see much of him at the house. Or here at the boatyard. It's really been an awful lot of fuss about nothing.'

'I'm glad to hear it,' said Ruth fervently. 'And you can trust me. I'll make sure everyone knows you're moving into another house.'

'I thought you would,' murmured Jilly drily as they turned off the road and into the entrance of the marina restaurant and bar.

CHAPTER SIX

By Friday afternoon Jilly was feeling tense and on edge. Her attempts to stay clear of Ed had been successful. The only times she had actually seen him had been at the boatyard when she had been passing through the yard and he had been at his boat. At the house she had managed to avoid him morning and night. She had a suspicion that it had been made easy to stay clear of him by his co-operation because although they were both actually in the house during the night, he hadn't come into the living-room or anywhere near the east wing. He had returned long after she had and had gone straight to the west wing and had stayed in his room all night. In the mornings he had always waited until she had gone to work before leaving his room.

But the strain taxed her nerves and emotions. Every night she had lain awake tensely aware that he was in the house and longing to be with him. Frustration had built up within her until her nerves had felt as if they had been tied into knots. If he had never touched her, had never kissed her she would have been able to cope, she argued with herself, but now she knew what it was like to be close to him. She knew that she would find comfort in his arms and release from tension.

Often she had tried to imagine what would have happened if she had left her tangled bed and had gone to his room, but fantasising had only increased the pain of frustration and had to be abandoned. She had tried getting up and reading. She had tried getting up and going to the kitchen and making herself a drink of warm milk, moving not quietly, but with as much clatter as she could in the hope of disturbing him, so that he would have come to find out what she had been doing. Nothing she had done had helped.

She had arranged to leave the house early Saturday morning to meet Irma at the Leonards' house so she went straight from work on Friday evening to the House of Doves to pack up her clothes and belongings. By ten o'clock she had packed and had carried everything down to the car to stow it in the boot and on the back seat. All she had left in the bedroom was her nightgown and a change of clothes for the morning. She vacuumed the bedroom carpet and, after taking a bath, she cleaned the bathroom. Then, sure she would go to sleep quickly after all her hard work, she went to bed, knowing that Ed had not yet returned.

For the first time that week she fell asleep as soon as her head touched the pillow and she might have slept all night if a noise hadn't woken her. Not quite sure what had penetrated the deep slumber into which she had sunk, she sat up listening. She heard nothing except the faint rustle of leaves of an oleander bush against the outer wall of the room.

Lying down again, she tried to sleep, but her mind was too alert. She was tense again, every nerve quivering as she listened and at the same time tried to recall what the noise that had disturbed her had sounded like. It had sounded like a door closing. The door of her bedroom closing. Quickly she sat up, reached out and snapped on the bedside lamp. Pale silvery grey walls, mirrors glinting, a yellow lizard seemingly transfixed on the wall opposite to her, its legs spread out, its eyes opaque, watching her warily. There was no one in the room except herself. Yet she was sure she had heard the door close.

Pushing back the sheet which was the only covering she had been using she slid off the bed and padded across to the bathroom. Light glittered on tiles and more mirrors. There was no one in the room.

For a moment she stood hesitating, listening again, then she left the room and went along the passage to the kitchen. All the lights were on and she knew who had left them on, she thought, with a twisted grin. Switching them off she went out into the hallway. The front door was wide open.

She stepped out and went down the shallow steps. The floodlights were not on for once, and the whole area was shadowy. Again she paused, listening. She could hear nothing but the sigh of the sea beyond the edge of the terrace. In the cloudless blue-black sky the moon sailed serenely almost on the wane now, sliding down towards an unseen horizon.

Warm air caressed her skin as, in her brief cotton sleeveless nightgown, she walked barefoot around the pool towards the protective railing at the edge of the cliffs. Was it only a week ago she had stood here and had looked out at the star-shimmered sea? A week since she had offered herself to Ed and had been rejected by him? If it were to happen again, if he were to come on to the terrace tonight she would behave in exactly the same way, she realised, because now she knew for sure that she was in love with him.

'Well, well, who is this, flitting about in a see-through nightie under the light of the moon,' said a deep mocking voice nearby.

'Aaah.' Jilly's scream was stifled by her own hands pressed against her mouth and she shook from head to foot with shock.

The aluminium legs of a lounger scraped on tiles. The deep voice cursed fluently. A dark figure swooped towards her and strong sinewy arms went around her. He drew her against him murmuring soft words of comfort. He was naked except for thin cotton sleeping shorts and the skin of his chest was warm and slightly sticky. Through the stuff of his shorts she could feel the powerful thrust of his maleness and felt the nerves in the lower part of her body quiver into arousal.

'I didn't mean to scare you,' he whispered, his head pressed against hers. 'I thought you'd seen me.'

The heat of his hands was scorching through the thin stuff of her nightgown and the feel of his arms holding her so closely was now more than comforting. He was holding her as if he would never let her go.

'I'm all right now,' she said a little shakily.

'But I'm not,' he said with a low laugh, and his hand slid up from her waist to cup her breast. 'You'll have to do something for me, now.'

Hands around his wrist she tried to drag his hand down.

'It's late,' she quavered. 'We should go back to bed.'

His swift smile glinted in the darkness of his face as he broke her hold on his wrist easily and raised both his hands to frame her face.

'I'm in total agreement with you. The problem is whose bed, yours or mine?' he whispered, his lips hovering close to hers.

'You've been drinking,' she accused, tilting her head back.

'A little. Enough to make me reckless but not enough to kill desire,' he murmured, 'As you must have noticed by now,' he added with wicked suggestiveness, and plundered her lips with his.

Stars danced in the darkness of her mind while her head reeled under the onslaught of his kiss and joyful laughter welled up within her as she acknowledged that this was what she had been longing for all week. Aroused by the feel of his skilful fingers caressing her as much as by the urgent thrust of his hips against hers she responded wholeheartedly, her fingers grasping his hair, holding his head down and his lips against hers when he would have moved away.

'This has been a hell of a week, wanting you and not having you,' he whispered when at last she let him free his mouth from the clinging softness of hers.

'For me too,' she sighed. 'Oh, don't stop now. Please don't stop now.'

'I wasn't thinking of stopping,' he replied with another low laugh. 'But like you I think we should go to bed to finish this behind a closed door where we won't be interrupted. Mine would be best.'

Holding her hand he led her around the pool and into the house and for once he didn't switch on all the lights. Through the shadowed kitchen and along the passage to the rooms in the west wing they went, pausing occasionally to kiss and cling.

A single lamp in the bedroom cast light across the wide bed revealing that his sheets were in a tangle too, suggesting that he also had been tossing and turning restlessly, and again she felt that sudden surge of joy because all through the week of tension and strain he had been wanting her as much as she had been wanting him.

'How silly we've both been,' she murmured when, after he had straightened the bed, they were lying close together on it. 'Pretending we didn't want to be with each other all week.'

'But just think how much more exciting getting together

is going to be because of our restraint,' he retorted. 'Are you going to take off that ridiculous nightgown yourself or should I help you?'

'I'd like to have your help,' she replied with a touch of shyness, her hands reaching out eagerly to slide his shorts down over his thighs.

His fingertips drifted over her body gently yet provocatively, sliding into hollows, tantalising delicate nerve endings until she throbbed with delight, arching against the hard muscularity of his body, exulting in the knowledge that it was she who had aroused in him a raw pulsing hunger he was only just holding in check.

'Nothing has changed since last Friday,' he said huskily as he slid over her. 'I still haven't had anyone. I've been saving it all for you. Are you ready?'

'More than ready,' she moaned, rubbing against him, inciting him even more by instinctive movements of her hips and breasts. She was high with desire, dizzy with it, smouldering with it.

The stars in the darkness of her mind swirled and exploded as his life-force entered the welcoming softness of her body, inviting her to join him in a violent eruption of new and exquisite sensations that were over all too soon. Tears spurted from her eyes and spattered his chest and face. She felt his lips kissing them away from her eyes and her cheeks.

'You are disappointed?' he whispered.

'Oh, no. Not at all. It was wonderful, but over so quickly.'

'I know. Because we were both impatient.' His laugh was gruffly mocking. 'And we were both more than ready.' Lying on his back he pulled her head down against his shoulder. 'We'll try again later, take our time to savour every moment.'

Tears still wetting her face she smiled and rubbed her cheek against him and slid an arm across his waist.

'This is good,' she murmured, 'to lie like this feeling contented, all the tension between us gone. I . . .' She stopped abruptly, biting her lower lip hard, all the pleasure of the aftermath of passion draining out of her. She had been going to say, 'I love you,' then had suddenly remembered that she mustn't say it to him.

'You,' he prompted, his voice thick and drowsy. He slid lazy fingers through the silky strands of her hair.

'I could stay here for ever,' she whispered, and that was almost like saying she loved him, she thought.

Fingers of apricot-coloured light, announcing the rising of the suns, were spreading across the sky before they both fell asleep. Slowly darkness retreated from the room revealing the two people lying on the wide luxurious bed, on the tangled sheet that half covered them, on the hand-carved beautiful furniture. In the other bedroom, the one in the east wing, the sun shone in directly, filling it with rosy light and causing the lizard to scurry from its nocturnal resting place on the wall to hide behind the dressing-table.

As the morning progressed the silent house seemed to stretch itself under the heat of the sun and in the garden birds flew about twittering. The pool winked and glittered. Down on the beach the waves chuckled.

Suddenly the silence was shattered by the shrill ring of a telephone bell. When no one answered it the bell went on ringing, persistently, annoyingly. In the west-wing bedroom Jilly heard it at last and stirred reluctantly, becoming aware of an unusual weight resting on her breast. Hair was tickling her throat and chin and the musky scent of it filled her nostrils. She opened her eyes as the telephone bell shrilled again and realised what the weight was. Ed was lying half on and half off her, his head against her breast.

She waited and listened, her head half lifted from the pillow. The telephone didn't ring again so smilingly she relaxed and lay back, closing her eyes. It was so good to be there with him lying against her, his left arm about her waist. She wanted to savour this moment too, as they had savoured every loving and titillating caress during the night. She wanted to indulge herself by pretending that he was wholly hers for ever.

The phone bell shrilled again, causing her to stiffen.

'Better answer it,' murmured Ed without moving.

'Yes,' she whispered. 'I'll go.'

She slid from under him and taking her nightgown from the floor slipped it over her head. The phone was still ringing when she reached the kitchen. Shaking back her tousled hair she lifted the receiver and spoke into the mouthpiece.

'Jilly?' Irma Stratton's voice was sharp. 'What the hell are you doing? I've been waiting at the Leonards' house to let you in. We said we'd meet here at ten. It's now ten-fifty.'

'I'm sorry. I . . . I slept in.' Jilly gasped. Today was the day she moved out, left this beautiful luxurious house where the doves cooed softly and peacefully in the morning. It was time to leave it. Time to leave its owner. But how could she leave him after last night? And how could he let her go, for that matter?

'I thought that must be what had happened.' Irma was sounding a little less annoyed. 'Come now. I'll wait for you. But get here before noon. I have guests coming for lunch.'

Irma hung up and Jilly returned the receiver to its rest. She didn't want to go but she supposed she would have to. It wasn't going to be easy explaining to Irma that she no longer wanted to move into the Leonards' house because she wanted to stay with Ed.

Whatever was she thinking of? She had to move out because another woman was coming to stay in that house. She had to move out because everyone would know she was having an affair with Ed if she didn't. Racing to her own bedroom she showered quickly, dried and dressed in the clothes she had laid out for herself. Then she stripped the bed and bundled the sheets into the laundry basket. Racing back to Ed's bedroom she went up to the bed. He was lying on his stomach, his broad sun-tanned back smooth and inviting to the touch. All she could see of his face was a corner of his jaw.

'Ed, I have to go,' she announced. 'I promised Irma I'd meet her at the Leonards' house. I'm late already.'

He didn't move and she went closer to the bed to bend over and look closely at him. Black lashes lay like a dark fan against all she could see of his cheek. He seemed to be sunk in a deep slumber.

She hadn't the heart to wake him up again. Wondering briefly if he had remembered he was supposed to drive to the airport to meet the French woman off the plane from Miami, she decided against waking him to remind him. After all he didn't know she knew about the woman coming and she didn't really have the right to tell him what to do. She didn't have any rights where he was concerned. None at all. Turning away she tip-toed from the room.

'I thought that you'd changed your mind when you didn't show up,' said Irma, coming down the steps of the Leonards' house when Jilly got out of her car in its driveway.

'Oh, no,' said Jilly, opening the back door of the car and

beginning to haul out her travelling-bags. Already the sun
was hot, beating down on her uncovered head. The white-
washed breeze blocks from which the house was built shone
pale gold. Scarlet hibiscus flowers made splashes of colour
against the walls and over the rail of the small veranda a
vine of purple bougainvillaea tumbled. She followed Irma
up the steps and through the double front door into the big
living-room where an overhead fan turned slowly.

'Now this key is for the front door and this is for the
back,' explained Irma as they stood in the kitchen which
was approached directly from the living-room through an
archway. 'The back door is there,' she said, pointing to it.
'There is also a key for the patio window that opens on to
the deck at the back of the house from the dining-room.'
They moved from the kitchen into the dining-room
through another archway. 'I think that you're going to find
this place much more cosy than the other house, with it
being smaller. And then you'll find that here you're among
some of your friends and acquaintances who work on the
yachts. Dick Markham is right next door.' Irma grimaced.
'Not that I think that's much of a plus. I hear he's given to
holding very rowdy all-night parties. I'll help you bring in
the rest of your stuff and then I really must fly. I'll talk to
you again about the materials for the curtains Ann
Leonard would like you to make.'

Once Irma had left Jilly lost no time in opening her cases
and hanging her clothes in the cupboard in the bigger
bedroom of the two bedrooms. It was a big airy room that
had its own bathroom and it was reached through a door at
the end of the living-room furthest away from and opposite
to the archway into the kitchen.

She wasn't going to think about what had happened last
night, she had decided. Thinking about it wouldn't help. It

was done, was over and the best thing she could do was to forget it. She was sure that was what Ed would do, especially when his guest arrived.

Yet all the time she was listening for the sound of a car approaching the house, hoping he would come after her. Several cars did come along the narrow lane on which the house was situated but none of them stopped in the short driveway.

She made herself some lunch, or rather brunch, and, realising that there was very little food in the fridge, she locked up the house and drove into Williamsburg. The big and only supermarket was packed with people, both native islanders and tourists, busy shopping for the weekend. It took her an hour to buy what she wanted and get through the check-out. She drove back to the Leonards' house and spent another hour restocking the fridge and food storage cupboards. Now, if anyone called on her, she was prepared. The next thing was to make up the bed.

But no one did call on her that afternoon or evening. The sun set, the stars came out, the moon began to rise. Cars crunched by along the lane and stopped at the house next door. Dick Markham was having a party, apparently. She didn't know him very well although he was one of the catamaran captains. If she had known him better she might have invited herself over to his party, just to while away the time.

Another restless, disturbed night passed by and she was sitting in the dining-room next morning wondering what she was going to do for the rest of the day when the phone rang. She rushed over to it, her heart beating wildly, but the voice which answered her breathless hello was Ruth's.

'All moved in?'

'Yes.'

'Then how about coming for a sail with us? We're going out with Gerry and Sue, to give them a big send-off, and then we'll stop at Pirate's beach for a picnic and sail back at sunset time. If you decide to come, meet us at the marina in half an hour.'

'OK.'

She packed her ice-box with food for the picnic and stuffed swimming and snorkelling gear into a canvas bag. After locking all the doors and making sure she had all the keys with her she left the house and drove out past the airport towards the town.

Several boats already had sails hoisted and were drifting towards the entrance of the harbour in the light breeze when she reached the marina. They were all clustered around the black-hulled, tan-sailed boat called *Black Diamond*. Running down the finger dock, Jilly leapt aboard Raoul's catamaran and at once it eased away from the marina under engine. After stowing her ice-box and canvas bag down below she went up to the main mast to help Ruth hoist the mainsail.

'I've told everyone you've moved out of the House of Doves,' Ruth said, once the sail was up and filling with wind. 'And I can't help feeling a certain gleeful satisfaction because you've given Ed Forster the cold shoulder. Must be a bit of a blow to his ego to have you moving out of his house. He's not used to rejection.'

'Isn't he? But I thought you turned him down, a couple of years ago,' said Jilly, her golden eyes opening wide with counterfeit surprise. 'You told me you did.'

Ruth didn't turn a hair, nor did her colour change but her eyes flickered and she looked away, beyond Jilly's shoulder.

'Oh, look there's Simon waving to you,' she said, 'I got

the impression he was quite put out when he heard that
you'd moved out of the House of Doves and that now he's
wishing he hadn't offered to crew for Gerry and Sue.'

Jilly turned. The big catamaran had soon caught up with
the rest of the fleet and she could see Simon quite clearly
standing on the foredeck of *Black Diamond*. She waved an
arm and he waved back. The catamaran surged closer to
the old black ketch until the bows of the boats were level.
Cupping his hands about his mouth Simon shouted,

'Sorry, Jilly. Do you forgive me?'

'Of course, I do,' she shouted back. 'Have a good trip
back.'

'I'll write to you. Who knows, I might come back here
sooner than you think,' he yelled.

'Heaven forbid,' murmured Ruth ungenerously as the
catamaran sailed past the ketch and out of shouting distance.

It was a lovely golden and blue day, a perfect sailing day
with the wind just strong enough to keep all the yachts
moving without the crews having to expend much energy.
The little fleet of friends and well-wishers escorted the *Black
Diamond* out of the harbour and around the north-western
tip of the island. They sailed past tourist-crowded beaches
of the big resorts and on past the big bight of Baie Jaune.
Through Raoul's binoculars Jilly observed the surf
thundering up the wide beach that rimmed the bay. There
were a few people on it. Slowly she raised the glasses until
she had them trained on the top of the cliffs at the eastern
end of the bay. All she could see of the House of Doves was
the red roof glowing through green foliage. While she was
looking the flock of doves that lived in the cliffs soared up,
like paper darts fluttering against the bright green of the
trees.

The fleet parted company with *Black Diamond* opposite

the house as the black ketch pointed her bows at the distant northerly end of the island of Angosta beyond which the Atlantic ocean rolled. The fleet sailed on in a leisurely fashion past the port Caracet, where pastel-pink and yellow houses with red roofs glinted amongst the foliage of palm trees and the broken walls of the old fort shimmered in the sunlight high on the headland.

Pirate's Bay was an almost landlocked pool of deep clear water. High hills covered with thick scrubby trees and tall cacti encircled the bay making it hard to approach from the land. The beach was pale yellow and firm. Beneath the surface of the water huge coral heads grew. After exploring among them Jilly helped Ruth take the food they had brought ashore and spent the rest of the afternoon lazily sunning herself.

They sailed back at sunset time, entering Town Bay just as the round red disc of the sun slipped below the horizon. Although invited by Raoul and Ruth to have dinner with them, Jilly declined. She wanted to get back to the Leonards' House just in case Ed decided to call on her.

He came when she was about to give up waiting and go to bed. She was sitting in the living-room watching a rather old American sit-com on the local TV channel when fingers rapping on a glass panel of the front door drew her attention. She looked round and felt her heart skip a beat as she recognised his shape through the window. She swung open the door.

'You forgot something.' he said and brought his right hand from behind his back. In it was her crumpled wisp of a nightgown. She must have left it lying on the bed in her bedroom at his house.

'Thank you.' She took it from him.

'It took me a while to find out where you'd gone,' he said

with a wry grin. 'I didn't like to be too obvious with my queries. I came earlier but you were out.'

'I went sailing with Ruth.' Her heart was beating so fast and loud she was sure he must be able to hear it. 'Won't you come in?'

'Not tonight. Some other time.' He gave her an underbrowed sultry glance which made her nerves quiver expectantly. 'See you around,' he added laconically.

He turned on his heel and went down the steps. Under the porch-light his dark hair shone, his white shirt glimmered. She felt her heart would burst.

'Ed,' she pleaded and he paused, shoulders stiffening, but he didn't turn. With his back to her he said with just a hint of exasperation in his voice,

'Well?'

Pride stepped in and prevented her from pleading any more. She must always remember she had no rights where he was concerned and never would have.

'I've finished repairing your jib,' she said, coolly businesslike. 'Shall I make a bag for it? Or do you already have a bag for it?'

'I have a bag,' he drawled, not turning round. 'I'll collect the sail from you at the end of the week. I'm hoping to launch the boat next Friday when Piet and I come back from Miami.'

'But what about your . . .' Fingers pressed against her mouth, she murmured the word 'guest' against them hoping he hadn't heard.

Slowly he turned to look at her.

'What did you say?' he drawled.

'Nothing. It doesn't matter. I hope you have a good time in Miami. Good night.'

She backed to the door, stepped into the living-room and

closed the door after her. After a while she heard his car
start up and drive away.

The false sound of a live audience's laughter startled her.
The television was flickering badly and the black-and-
white pictures of people were distorted. She stepped over
and switched it off and becoming aware of the nightgown
in her hand she went into the kitchen to put it in the
washing machine with the few clothes she had collected in
it ready to wash the next evening.

How, after all they had been to each other on Friday
night, could he be so coolly off-hand, so apparently
untouched? Because he was a man, was the answer that first
sprung to mind, only to be rejected. Kevin had been a man
too, but he hadn't been so stiff and wary. But then Kevin
had loved her and hadn't been afraid to say so. Kevin
hadn't cared if she had known he loved her. Kevin hadn't
been afraid of commitment, at least not of commitment to
her, and Ed was. Ed was afraid of commitment to anyone.
Why?

More than ever she was convinced his sensibilities had
been seared when he had been younger. Who had hurt
him? The woman he had eloped with? Had he really
eloped with someone else's wife? Or had Irma been right
when she had drily suggested he had made up that story to
impress the vulnerable and romantic widow he had found
living in his house?

The next day was chaotic at the boatyard. With Piet
away Jilly had to help Marcha in the office and chandlery,
leaving the island girl, Cora, to work in the sail-loft. The
telephone bell seemed to ring incessantly as yachtsmen
called to find out if the equipment they required was
stocked in the chandlery. Two lots of sails were brought in
for repair and the harbour master's wife came to ask Jilly to

make her some curtains. It was hard to get away for lunch and in the end they decided to keep the office open and go at different times so that there was always someone there to answer the phone. Marcha went first, returning at half-past one to let Jilly walk along to the marina restaurant to grab a sandwich and a drink.

When Jilly returned to the office an elegant woman, whose swathed dress of red and blue silk shrieked of Paris, was just about to leave.

'Wait one moment, *madame*,' Marcha said. 'Here is Jilly Carter now so we can check with her that she gave Edouard the note. Jilly, this is Madame Paulette Lavalle from France. You remember I gave you a message to give to Ed about the time of her arrival. Did you give it to him?'

'Yes, I did. That same evening.' Jilly surveyed the French woman. About forty years of age, she was well preserved, but she looked very annoyed. Irritation was pinching in the corners of her lips, giving them a downward turn.

'Are you sure he read the note, Madame Carter?' asked Paulette Lavalle, raising her arched eyebrows. She spoke English with a very strong French accent.

'Quite sure. Why do you ask?'

Paulette's dark brown eyes which were such a striking contrast with her smoothly-coiffured gilt-coloured hair blinked and she glanced away. A slight smile curved her lips and she shrugged. Yet in spite of the smile and the shrug Jilly had the impression the woman was seething with rage.

'It is not important. Thank you so much, *mesdames*.'

She walked from the office closing the door behind her. Jilly turned to look at Marcha.

'What was that all about?'

'He didn't meet her when she arrived,' said Marcha. 'So

she thinks that maybe it is my fault. That I didn't give him the message.'

'You think Ed excused himself by blaming you,' exclaimed Jilly.

'I don't know and I don't much care. I'm not at all sorry Ed stood her up by not meeting her. I don't like her and never have,' said Marcha.

'You've met her before?'

'Some years ago. She and I were both much younger then than we are now,' said Marcha with a grin. 'I don't think she recognised me. But I knew her right away. She has preserved herself very well.'

'Where did you meet her? In France?'

'No, no. Why would I ever go to France?' Marcha leaned back in her office chair and swung in it gently. The light coming through the windows reflected in her glasses.

'For a holiday,' suggested Jilly.

'Always my family take me to Holland or to the States for any vacation,' said Marcha. 'I met her here on the island at a party up at the House of Doves.' Her lips twitched into a smile of reminiscence. 'One of Ed's wild parties,' she murmured. 'What fun we used to have. I remember Paulette was there with her first husband, Pierre Martin.'

'Martin,' Jilly repeated slowly. 'This Pierre wouldn't have been related to Michelle, would he?'

'He was brother to Michelle's and Ed's mother. He was their uncle. He left the island and went to work and live in France. He met Paulette there. Do you know that Ed's grandfather still lives in Caracet? He used to work for the French Government, in the customs and immigration offices.'

'Yes, I met Monsieur Martin at the House of Doves one

day when he was visiting Ed,' replied Jilly. 'I was introduced to him.'

'That was an unusual thing for Ed to do. He usually likes to keep his mother's family in the background. And most of them don't like to associate with him too much after the way he behaved with Paulette.'

'How did he behave?' asked Jilly, but thought she knew the answer to that question already.

'When Pierre and Paulette returned to France after their holiday Ed followed them there. Well, not exactly followed them but he went to France to take some courses there in naval architecture at one of their schools. Pierre made him very welcome in his home, since Ed was his sister's son, and Ed repaid the hospitality by eloping with Paulette to the French Riviera. Pierrre shot himself.'

'Oh, no,' Jilly gasped.

'Didn't kill himself, fortunately, but made the point that he had been betrayed by his young wife and his even younger nephew. It was quite a scandal in the small French town where Pierrre and Paulette lived.'

'But what happened afterwards?' asked Jilly.

'No one really knows for sure except that Pierre divorced Paulette.'

'Ed has never said anything about what happened?'

'No, not to anyone here, as far as I know, but then he didn't come here for a long time after it had happened. He only returned here after his father's death when he and Michelle inherited the house. And now that woman is here again. I don't really blame Ed for not meeting her off the plane or not being at home when she called on him at the House of Doves.'

'So she isn't staying with him?'

'No. She and her husband are staying at the International Hotel. She left another message for him. She wants him to call on her when he returns from Miami.'

'How did she know she could contact him here?' asked Jilly.

'Who knows? He was in France last year before the Transatlantic Race. Maybe they met then.' Marcha straightened up in her chair and became again the brisk businesslike person she was. 'But that's enough time wasted on trying to figure out what Ed is up to. Just you be glad you got out of his house before Paulette Lavalle turned up. I tell you that woman spells trouble with a capital T and we can only hope that Ed is now tough enough to deal with her. We don't want him involved in any more scandals. It wouldn't be good for business.'

'I wouldn't be too sure about that,' said Jilly with a grin. 'Just think of the free publicity you would get if he eloped with Paulette again and her second husband shot himself.'

'That sort of publicity I for one can do without,' said Marcha sternly, and then sighed. 'You know having Ed Forster as a business partner is very hazardous. There is no way you can guess what he is going to do next. God knows what sort of mischief he'll lead Piet into while they're in Miami. Sometimes I wish he'd never come back to this island and yet I know that without his backing Piet and I wouldn't have such a good business as we have today.' The telephone rang. Marcha made a face and picked up the receiver. 'Block's Boatyard,' she said. 'Can I help you?'

Jilly wandered into the stock-room and began to climb the ladder to the sail-loft. It was time she checked on what Cora was doing. She was conscious of a mixture of feelings. In one way she felt vaguely light-hearted because she had learned that there wasn't a woman staying at the House of Doves with Ed. She was also relieved that Ed hadn't invented the story of his elopement with a married woman just to impress her. He had, as he had said at the time, wanted her to know the truth about him.

But she also felt she was worried because Paulette Lavalle had turned up. Like Marcha she felt the woman spelled trouble for Ed. The gilt-haired, dark-eyed woman reminded her of someone; someone she had met recently. It wasn't until later in the day that she decided whom Paulette resembled, not in looks, but in manner. There was about Paulette the same predatory attitude possessed by Gloria Presensky.

CHAPTER SEVEN

BEING involved with the running of the boatyard with Marcha while Piet was away, Jilly had little time to think about personal problems. Only when she was alone at night in bed did she open up her mind to admit them.

Sometimes she had doubts about what she had done but mostly she was glad she had lost control over the surging sexual attraction she had felt towards Ed when they had met in the moonlight on the terrace at the House of Doves, and she found herself looking forward to his return from Miami with an excitement that had been lacking in her life for a long time.

She knew that he and Piet had returned on Friday afternoon because she heard their voices in the office but when she went down from the sail-loft at five p.m. neither of them was there.

On the drive back to the Leonards' house she stopped off at the supermarket, turning from the main road into the large car-crammed parking-lot beside the building. Finding an empty parking-space she glanced in the rear-view mirror before making a turn into the space and her heart leapt with joy. The grey Mustang convertible was right behind her, Ed at its wheel, his black hair lifting above his broad forehead, his shoulders straight and taut under a white shirt.

She parked, got out of the car and looked around but couldn't see him anywhere. Not until she was walking along the aisle between the refrigerated goods and the greengrocery stalls did she find him. He was there right in the middle of the narrow aisle, a cart containing only packs of beer and bottles of wine before him, and he was talking or rather listening to Paulette Lavalle who was holding a basket in front of her.

Jilly back-tracked, pulling her cart back. Behind her there was a yelp. She turned. A big brown-skinned woman in a brightly coloured shift with a red bandana tied around her crinkly black hair glared at her with big brown eyes.

'Just you watch what you's doin', missus,' she growled.

'Sorry,' said Jilly. 'I can't go forward. There's someone in the way and I can't get round him.'

'Well, you just tell him to get out of the way,' said the woman, and raising her voice she yelled. 'Hey you, man, move over and let us decent women pass.'

Ed looked up, his grin flashed and he stepped to one side, pulling his cart with him. Paulette moved too. She and Ed stood close together beside the glass doors of the one of the refrigerators.

'On you go, missus,' ordered the brown woman and Jilly pushed her cart on, her head high as she refused to glance at Ed and Paulette, pretending she hadn't seen them or recognised them. She didn't get very far. A big sun-tanned hand reached out and grabbed the handle of her cart and it was jerked sideways. She had to go with it. As the island woman pushed past her she was pressed against Ed's cart. She looked up at him from under scowling brows. He gave her one of his singularly sweet smiles and her knees wobbled as her bones seemed to melt in a familiar way.

'Have you got all you want, sweetheart?' he asked, his voice drawling with amusement. 'This is Jill, Paulette. I was just telling you about her.'

Sweetheart! In front of Paulette Lavalle! Sweetheart! In

a public place like a supermarket! What had got into him?

'Madame Carter and I have already met,' Paulette was saying with her rather exaggerated French accent. Jilly looked at her. The woman looked as if she had received a great shock. Her face was pale beneath the make-up, but she was recovering quickly. Forcing a smile, she said, 'André and I would be so pleased if you would both come to have dinner with us tonight at our hotel. We leave in the morning for Guadeloupe and will not have the chance again to talk with you.'

'Thanks for the invitation, but I believe you're having some friends over this evening for a barbecue, aren't you, Jill?' Ed said smoothly.

It was true. She had invited her new neighbours to a little house-warming party.

'Yes. Sorry I can't accept, Madame Lavalle,' she said, and with a hard shove she managed to push her cart forward. 'Excuse me, I must finish my shopping,' she added, and with a polite smile and nod to Paulette she pushed past Ed without looking at him.

'Don't bother to get any more beer or wine, darling,' Ed called after her. 'I've plenty here.'

Furious with him for assuming he could use her as a shield to protect himself from Paulette, Jilly didn't stop for any more purchases but went straight to the check-out counter that had the shortest line-up. Blindly she paid for what she had bought without making sure that the girl at the cash register had punched in the right amounts and without checking her change, something she usually did, having learned the hard way that islanders were notoriously inaccurate about numbers and when dealing with money.

She hurried out to her car and didn't even stop to buy

limes or bananas as she usually did from the country-women, who sat in the shade of the building on the edge of the road with their fresh produce spread about them. She was too angry with Ed.

How dared he put on a show like that? How dared he tell Paulette he was having an affair with her, for that was what she guessed he had been telling the Frenchwoman about. Fuming, she drove back to the Leonards' house vowing that if he dared to come and see her she would tell him, in no uncertain terms, what she thought of his behaviour in the supermarket.

He didn't come to the party, which was a relief. He didn't come until after midnight when everyone had gone and she was in the bedroom changing into her nightgown. Hearing the slight rattle of the knob of the front door as he turned it, she rushed into the living-room. Without turning away from her, watching her with the slightest glimmer of a smile in his eyes, he kicked the door shut behind him and stepped towards her, seeming bigger than usual in a suit of fine cream-coloured alpaca, the jacket open over a navy blue shirt.

She raised a fist as if to strike at him. He caught her wrist and laid her hand against his chest. Under her fingers she felt the throb of his heart through the thin cotton. The lean sun-bronzed face came down to hers. The blue eyes blazed into hers like laser beams and all her anger against him evaporated. His parted lips covered hers in a hungry kiss that seemed to blister her mouth.

'It's been another hellish week,' he muttered tautly when the kiss was over.

'For me too,' she sighed happily, and he scooped her up in his arms as if she had been a bunch of feathers.

'Which way?' he asked and she pointed to the open door of the bedroom.

Later, as they lay together in the darkness, she asked him about Paulette.

'The woman in the supermarket. I know she's the one you eloped with,' she whispered.

'Who told you?' he asked, stiffening warily.

'Marcha. Madame Lavalle came to the boatyard looking for you. She wanted to know why you hadn't met her off the plane last Saturday. Did you forget to go and meet her?'

'No. I didn't want to meet her and I can't understand why she wanted me to.'

'Perhaps she wanted to resurrect old times,' suggested Jilly drily. 'Why didn't you stay together after you eloped?'

'That is a question I'm not prepared to answer right now, sweetheart.' Mockery rippled through his voice as he kissed her temple, then her cheeks, his hand moving up from her waist stealthily to cup her breast. 'What happened between Paulette and me happened a long time ago and has nothing to do with you and me. Forget her and concentrate on us. This something, whatever it is between you and me, is very new, very different for me. Don't spoil it by asking questions. Just enjoy. We'll keep it secret. That should be easy now that you don't live in the same house as me.'

'But Paulette will tell everyone,' she argued. 'You told her about us. I know you did. The nerve of you calling me sweetheart and darling in front of her!'

'You should have seen the expression on your face,' he said, his laughter muffled against her shoulder. 'If looks could kill I'd be dead right now. Paulette won't say anything to anyone. I asked her not to. She understands the value of secrecy. No one better.' Bitterness grated briefly in his voice. 'And tomorrow she'll be gone. We'll probably never meet her again. Now where were we?'

'You were telling me just to enjoy,' she whispered, putting an arm around him and sliding her fingers over the small of his back. 'It's going to be hard keeping it a secret.'

'But very necessary if we don't want it spoiled by everyone talking about us,' he whispered urgently. 'I don't want people like Ruth Burrows sniping at us. I don't want people sneering at you. I have to protect your good name somehow. I should leave you alone, not come to see you, not make love to you ever again, but I don't think I can. I want you so much.'

'And I don't want you to leave me alone or not come to see me,' she replied, holding him closely. 'I want you so much, too. But how are we going to hide our feelings for each other? How can we avoid betraying ourselves at the boatyard?'

'We can easily ignore each other there, pretend we're not at all interested in each other, by not speaking to each other if we can avoid it. As for the rest we won't ever dine out at the same places or go to the same parties. Should be easy enough since we move in different circles. We'll meet only here, late at night when I can come. Just leave the front door unlocked when you go to bed at night so that I can get in without having to knock,' he said.

'So that you can steal in like a thief in the night,' she couldn't help teasing him.

'Like a lover,' he growled low in his throat and kissed her mercilessly until she had no desire to talk as passion boiled within her and overflowed.

She had to admit she found a certain impish delight in keeping their meetings a secret, ignoring him during the day at the boatyard, pretending she wasn't at all interested

in him. Pretending there was nothing between them added
a certain spice to their meetings. At first he came only on
Friday evenings as if in celebration of that first night
together at the House of Doves. Then he began to come
more often. He never came when she had visitors, nor after
he had given a party at the House of Doves. They never
attended the same social occasions.

One night after he had been particularly loving and they
were lying together in contented silence she dared to ask a
question.

'Are you happy?' she whispered.

'There is nowhere I'd rather be than here, right now,' he
murmured, rubbing his cheek against her breast.

'Have you ever felt like this before in your life?'

He laughed softly and raising his head kissed her lips as if
to silence her.

'What would you like me to say?' he scoffed. 'That you
are the only woman in the world for me?'

'Would it be so hard to say?' she challenged.

It was a mistake. She sensed that immediately, because he
stiffened and moved away from her, turning his back to
her.

'Don't push it,' he murmured. 'Be content to know that I
like being with you and that is why I come to see you so
often. You're very sweet and generous, more generous than
any woman I have ever known before, but try not to want
too much from me. I'm too old now to change. Accept that
and you won't be disappointed or hurt.'

She tried very hard to do what he suggested, to look
neither forwards nor backwards. She knew that their close
association was having an effect on her, that her fine skin
had a certain glow that hadn't been put there by sunshine,
that her eyes shone with a serenity that had been lacking in

them since Kevin had been killed. She was also aware that he had awakened in her a sensuality she would have never guessed she possessed, and often during the day, when she did encounter him accidentally in the office or when crossing the boatyard, she had difficulty in restraining the desire to touch him or to smile at him invitingly.

The sunshine-filled days went by and February slid into March. One morning towards the end of March she realised that she hadn't seen Ed in the yard or in the office for nearly three days, nor had he come to see her at night, even though, as always, she had left the front door unlocked for him to get in. When she left the sail-loft that evening she stopped in the office to ask Marcha where he was, not caring whether Marcha was surprised by her question.

Marcha answered the question with her usual end-of-the-day brusqueness.

'He's gone to California.'

'Why?'

'To keep an eye on his business there. He owns a yacht-designing and building company there. This little company is just a sideline for him. He only came in with Piet and me to help me out when we were getting started.'

'Will he be coming back?' Jilly felt suddenly very cold. Could he have left without telling her because he wanted to end their affair?

'His boat is here, isn't it?' said Marcha drily. 'He will come back for that, if for nothing else.'

Jilly couldn't help feeling hurt because Ed hadn't told her that he would be away for a while. Did it mean he wasn't very serious about his relationship with her? She tried telling herself not to take it so seriously either, to be like some of her women friends who were quite casual about their affairs with the men they lived with, reminding herself that she had no rights where he was concerned. But she missed him terribly and longed for him to return.

She tried to distract herself by spending more time at the marina bar after work, where her friends off the charter yachts and catamarans usually met, putting off for as long as she could her return to the Leonards' house because she dreaded the long, hot nights listening for the rattle of the front doorknob.

He came back when she had almost given up hope, when she had convinced herself that the affair was over. Three weeks he had been gone. It was already the middle of April and the sun was on its way from the Equator to the Tropic of Cancer, just five and half degrees of latitude north of St Mark's. At noon the temperature was much higher than it had been, and as a result tempers were often higher too.

Sometimes, aching to be with Ed, she had found the nights unbearably uncomfortable. There was no air-conditioning in the Leonards' house and the overhead fans only moved warm air about, they did not really create any cool breeze. With the increase in the temperature her emotions had begun to swing wildly and often she felt a resentment towards Ed she might not have felt in a more temperate climate.

He wasn't worthy of her love, she would argue with herself, so why should she burn herself out pining for him? And there were times she felt she hated him more than loved him; hated him for having made love to her; hated him for having made her his mistress. Then she would start to hate herself for having let him become so important to her.

She was actually in bed one night when he came at last. In an instant she was out of bed and running, joy leaping within her, all her resentment temporarily forgotten. She met him in the doorway that led into the living-room and stopped short, one hand against her heart as if she would stop its excited throb.

'Miss me?' he asked, and the blaze in his eyes belied the light mocking lilt in his voice.

'Now why would I miss you?' she countered, tipping back her head and giving him a disdainful stare. 'You really have a most overbearing conceit.'

'That's just the sort of greeting I like to hear. Lets me know where I stand in your estimation,' he retorted with a low laugh, and one arm about her waist swept her with him into the bedroom.

'No, wait, Ed. Please wait.' She turned to him, tried to push him away. 'We must talk.'

'Sure, but later. First things first,' he whispered thickly, and his fingers digging into her buttocks through the thin stuff of the nightgown, he kissed her hard, bruising her lips. Her neck aching from the pressure she tried to resist but, as always, his kisses and caresses overcame her misgivings and her body leapt and quivered to his demands. Soon they were lying on the bed and for a while it was as if he had never been away.

In the hot, scented darkness all inhibitions fled and they each found new ways to express their passion for each other. Filled with a wild urgency to convince him that she wanted to be the only woman in his life, she touched and tasted him everywhere she could, arousing in him a fierce response that he couldn't hold in check, and he possessed her with a loud shout of primitive pleasure, urging her to join him in the soaring explosive sensation that carried them both beyond resentment and jealousy. Never before had the culmination of passion seemed so sweet or complete to Jilly. Lying in his arms, bathed in sweat yet feeling voluptuously drowsy, she admitted to him how much she had really missed him and added cautiously,

'Marcha says you have been in California and that you have a business there.'

'That's so.' He was as laconic as ever.

'I wish you'd told me before you went that you would be away for so long and why,' she murmured. He didn't say anything so she went on, 'Will you be going back there?'

He was silent for so long that she began to wish she hadn't asked the question, but he didn't turn away from her and her held breath came out in an audible sigh of relief when he answered slowly,

'I'll be going back there, probably at the beginning of May. Most years I spend all the summer and autumn there. What about you? Where will you go this summer? Back to England, I would suggest. It isn't good to stay on the island when you're not accustomed to the heat. It gets as hot as Hades.'

'I know,' she whispered. She was finding it hard to speak because her throat was aching. He was going to leave the island. He was going to California for the summer and autumn and he hadn't asked her to go with him. What was more, he didn't want her to go with him. She guessed that he didn't or he wouldn't have suggested she go to England.

He would be leaving around the beginning of May. In ten days' time. She had ten days to convince him that he loved her enough not to leave her behind when he left, enough to ask her to go with him. She turned to him, snuggling her softness against his hardness.

'I could go to stay near San Francisco instead of going to England. Cindy Chandler, who crews on one of the schooners, has often invited me to go and stay with her at her parents' ranch. It's somewhere north of Oakland. I could come to see you, if you'd tell me where your business is. Or where you live when you're in California.'

'You could,' he agreed but he didn't sound very encouraging and he didn't tell her where his business was or where he lived when he was in California.

'But you would rather I didn't,' she said, giving in to the disappointment she felt, which seemed to be rising up in her like a fever, distorting her emotions. 'You would rather I went to England, thousands of miles away from you.'

'I didn't say that,' he pointed out coolly.

'No, but you implied it. Like the business you're in with Piet and Marcha here, I'm only a sideline,' she said in a low voice that shook with anger because he seemed so cruelly indifferent. 'Someone in whom you've invested a little of your time but who is not the most important person in your life. In fact I doubt if any person, male or female, is important to you. You care only for yourself, and what you like doing. That trimaran out there in the harbour is more important to you than I am or any other person. You're the most selfish person I've ever met.'

He didn't say anything but she heard a sharp intake of breath indicating his impatience with her. Then he moved, sat up and slid to the edge of the bed. The bedside lamp clicked on. Shafts of light shone on his bare bronzed back then he was gone, into the shadows. Feeling a strange kind of panic surging through her she sat up.

'What are you doing?' she asked.

'Can't you guess?' he drawled mockingly. 'I'm getting dressed.'

'But why? Where are you going?' she demanded, panic making her voice more shrill than usual. He had never left her before sunrise before.

Tucking the tail of his shirt into the waist-band of his

trousers he came out of the shadows and towards the bed. He rested his fists on the mattress, and supported by straight arms leaned towards her. By the light of the lamp she could see his lean face was set in hard lines. His eyes were as cold as northern seas.

'You seem to be forgetting the ground-rules of this arrangement of ours,' he said softly. 'We don't ask each other questions as to where, when and why. I'm going because I don't want to skirmish with you tonight while you're in this over-excited mood. If I stay we'll quarrel and I don't want that to happen. I've warned you before not to push me or to try and change me. Let it be as it was before I went away.'

'But I can't let it be as it was before you went away, I can't,' she cried.

'In that case we'd best call it quits,' he said stonily and, straightening up, he turned away.

She caught up with him just before he reached the front door. With a sheet wrapped toga-wise about her she slid between him and the door and spread her arms wide across the panels.

'I'm sorry, sorry, sorry,' she gasped. 'Please don't go like this, I'll be quiet. I won't ask questions, I promise.'

His face softened fractionally and his eyes almost lit up with a smile. Raising a hand he curved his fingers to the shape of her cheek and then slid them into her hair.

'You will, and I'll resent them. Best for us to cool off for a while,' he murmured.

He bent his head and kissed her. His lips were hard and didn't linger. She sensed in the brevity of the kiss, in its lack of tenderness, his wish to be done with her for a while.

'You'll come again? On Friday?' she asked, aware of a terrible ache starting up within her.

Putting his hands on either side of her waist he moved her sideways and away from the door.

'I'm not making any promises that I might not be able to keep,' he replied curtly. 'I'll come when I can as I always have.'

He opened the door then pressed the button in the knob to the locked position and gave her a wicked sidelong glance.

'Just so that another thief can't steal in,' he mocked and went out, closing the door firmly behind him.

Stunned and chilled by his departure, Jilly leaned against the wall beside the door, listening to his car start up and drive away. After a while she moved and trudged into the kitchen, to fill the kettle. If she went back to bed she would only toss and turn, full of regrets because she hadn't been able to hold her tongue, so she might as well make herself some tea.

Sitting at the dining-room table, she drank tea and tried to analyse what had happened. He had seemed so happy to be with her, so close that she had believed the time to be right to move their relationship a little further forward. Perhaps he was right, it would do them both good to cool off a little. But they had been apart for three weeks already. Hadn't that been enough cooling-off time, enough time to find out how they really felt about each other?

The trouble was, the kind of affair he wanted, casual and secretive, didn't suit her temperament. She wanted to be more than just the woman he came to see when he was on the island. She wanted commitment, permanence. So perhaps, as he had said, it would be best to call it quits. If he loved her he would never have made such a suggestion. If he loved her he would have wanted her to visit him in California.

Next morning she felt much better than she had expected. The sparkle of sunlight on the water, the deep azure blue of the sky, even the usual joshing of her by Piet about her lateness did much for her spirits. The world wouldn't come to an end if Ed didn't come to see her any more. She would survive in the same way she had survived the shock of Kevin's death.

During the next ten days she saw very little of Ed. No longer was there any need to pretend she had no interest in him, to avoid speaking to him, because he was never in the office or in the boatyard when she passed through. And he didn't once come to see her, even though she left the front door unlocked when she went to bed.

Once again she tried to blot out all thoughts or memories of him by being more sociable, but with the end of April fast approaching a change was coming over the island. Yachts that had been anchored in the harbour or tied up at the marina for the winter season were leaving every day, their crews taking them north for the summer season in the north-eastern United States. Businesses were closing now that fewer tourists were flooding the streets and the big cruise-ships had stopped calling at the port. At the boatyard there was little to do. No one wanted sails repairing or awnings made. Jilly filled up her working hours by making the curtains for the Leonards' house, and many of her evenings re-upholstering some of the furniture.

The sparkle gradually went from the mornings. Often a heat haze hung over the sea and the mountains, and sometimes squalls of rain hit the island, dancing over the corrugated roofs, obliterating views of mountains with curtains of slanting grey water, and sending people scurrying for shelter. The rain storms lasted only a few minutes and afterwards the pavements and roadways would steam as the sun re-appeared.

Friday came around again, the last Friday in April. Lingering in the office that morning talking to Marcha, Jilly noticed a movement through the window behind Marcha's desk. Three people were walking by slowly, on their way to the dock where the tenders for some of the yachts in the harbour were tied up. Piet and Ed and one other, a tall blonde woman in brief white shorts and a red shirt.

'Who is that with Piet and Ed?' Jilly asked abruptly.

Marcha swung her swivel-chair round and glanced out of the window.

'That is Carol Stacey. She and her family are staying at the House of Doves. Been there for a while now, ever since Ed came back from California. They are from San Francisco.' Marcha swung back. 'It's rumoured that she and Ed are going to be married,' she added.

'Really?' Shock made Jilly feel sick. 'When?'

'When he goes back to California, I suppose. He's flying there next week.' Marcha gave Jilly an underbrowed glance. 'She was at a party Piet and I went to, over in Caracet. Her father is very wealthy, a banker I believe, so I would think the wedding will be one of those big splurges and will be written up in the society columns of all the leading American papers. If it ever takes place.' Marcha's thin dark face expressed cynicism. 'Only when I read about it and see pictures of it will I believe Ed has got married to someone like her. He hates publicity. Had enough of it, I suppose, when his father was alive.'

'He hasn't said anything about getting married, then?' asked Jilly. She was recovering now, not feeling quite so sick. She went over to the window to see where Ed and the blonde woman had gone. They had reached the dock and were getting into the red Zodiac dinghy that belonged to Ed and which was tender to his trimaran. Soon it was bouncing across the water in the direction of the blue three-hulled boat with the glinting gold masts. Ed was taking Carol Stacey to see his boat. Jealousy flooded through Jilly. He had never taken her to see it.

'Not a word. But then you know what he's like, never says anything about what he's planning to do. We're lucky to have been told that he's thinking of going to California again,' said Marcha sardonically. 'But Michelle has mentioned that there might be a marriage in the family soon. She seems to be all for it. She's back you know. The film she was going to act in isn't going to be made after all. Had to be packed in because of lack of funds. You're not looking too good, Jilly. Heat getting to you already?'

'A little. I was wondering if you and Piet would mind if I went to England soon. My sister is getting married at the beginning of June and I was going to fly over then but now I think I'd like to go sooner, help to make her wedding-dress. There doesn't seem to be much going on here and . . .'

'Of course we wouldn't mind. Leave when you want, only stay over this weekend and Monday. Monday is carnival day and we'll be closed for the day. It's in celebration of the Queen of the Netherlands' birthday. Come over to our place and watch the parade. There'll be floats and bands and dancing. This year everyone is dressing up as packs of cards and the costumes will be very colourful.'

'I'd like to do that,' said Jilly. 'Do you think I could leave on Tuesday?'

'Sure. Go now to the travel agents and see if you can make a reservation,' said Marcha practically.

Jilly needed no more urging. She couldn't stay any

longer. Ed had meant it when he had said let's call quits. And now she knew why. He was going to marry the beautiful tall blonde girl, Carol Stacey. No wonder he hadn't wanted her to go and stay in San Francisco or visit him in California. No wonder he had wanted their affair to be a secret.

But to stay on the island knowing that he was there but was going to marry someone else would be worse than being in Felton had been after Kevin was killed.

She had no difficulty in booking a seat on a plane flying directly to Holland, from where she would be able to fly to England. The reservation made and the ticket issued, she cabled her parents telling them she would be in London on Wednesday and would phone them from there to tell them when she would arrive in Portsmouth. Then she went to see Irma Stratton to tell her she would be leaving the Leonards' house.

'Going home? Well, I don't really blame you. Not much to do here in the summer. When will you be coming back?' asked Irma curiously.

'I'm not sure. I might not come back.'

'Oh. I thought you liked it here.'

'I do ... well, I did. It's just that ... people change.'

'You can say that again,' sighed Irma. 'You've heard I suppose that Michelle is back and that she and Ed are going to sell the House of Doves to a guy from California? Yet they always said they would let me sell the house for them if they wanted to get rid of it. I know so many clients from the States who would pay millions to get hold of that place. I can't help feeling they have let me down.' Irma's lined face expressed petulance.

'Why are they selling it?' asked Jilly.

'They're short of cash, I guess,' said Irma with a shrug.

'But . . . I thought they were both wealthy,' said Jilly in bewilderment. 'Their father must have left them a lot of money.'

'The only thing of any value Jon Forster possessed was that house,' said Irma drily. 'The rest of his estate went to pay off his horrendous debts when he died. Michelle's career as an actress has hardly been productive to date. And everyone knows that the boat-design and building business isn't terribly lucrative. Ed spends all his money on those boats he races. Anyway the story is that Clark Stacey is going to buy the house for a cool three million dollars and Ed is going to marry Stacey's only daughter Carol to keep the house in the family, so to speak.'

'How awful,' whispered Jilly, thinking sadly of the lovely house where she had met Ed.

'How right you are. It is awful,' muttered Irma. 'To think of the commission I could have earned if they had let me sell it for them. I could have got more for it, I know I could.'

'So what shall I do about the keys to the Leonards' house?' asked Jilly. She had had enough of the American's concern about how many dollars she had lost through not having been the agent for the selling of the House of Doves.

'Why don't I come for them Tuesday morning before you go to the airport, and I'll lock up after you. What are you going to do with your car?'

'It really belongs to the business, so Piet will pick it up from the airport after I've gone,' said Jilly, rising to her feet. 'I must go now and finish off the upholstery on one of the armchairs. They look much better, I think the Leonards will be pleased.'

She was rescued from what might have been the most tedious Sunday of her life by Ruth and Raoul, who invited her to go with them on the catamaran to the island of

Angosta for a last sail before the boat was hauled out of the water for its annual repairs and paint job. As they left the harbour they passed close to Ed's trimaran, so close that Jilly was able to see its name painted on the stern of the central hull, *Blue Devil*.

'Have you heard the latest?' Ruth shouted to her above the rushing sound of water. 'The great lover has been netted at last. Who would have believed it? He's marrying for money. Those must be his future in-laws on board with him now. She's one of those tall golden Californian girls, with lots of white teeth that she shows a lot.'

Jilly said nothing. After glancing over at the trimaran and seeking and finding black hair shining in the sunlight and wide shoulders under a taut white shirt, she moved away from Ruth to find someone less abrasive.

The *Blue Devil* was still on its mooring when they returned at sunset, when the tops of the hills were tinted orange and the valleys were full of purple shadows. And it was still there next day when she arrived at Marcha and Piet's apartment to watch the parade go by from their balcony that overlooked Front Street. She had half hoped Ed would be among the group of people they had invited to watch the parade with them. Even if he had been accompanied by Carol Stacey, she would have liked to be able to tell him that she was leaving the island the next day and going back to England. But he wasn't there and he didn't come.

One more night with the front door of the Leonards' house unlocked in case he came. But in her heart she knew he wouldn't. It hurt terribly that he hadn't told her himself that he was going to marry and that was his real reason for ending their affair. Never could she excuse him for that bit of deceit.

She packed her cases methodically. She intended to take all her belongings with her in case she didn't return to the island. Once she was back in England, in the coolness of an English spring, she would look hard probably with surprise at her torrid tropical affair with Edouard Forster, sailor and lover. She would see it for what it had been, a product of the tropical climate and romantic surroundings, of sharing for a short while a beautiful house with its handsome, unpredictable owner. Like a tropical flower the affair had blossomed quickly under the hot sun and had faded just as fast.

The night passed quietly. She missed the sound of the wind rustling the bushes beside the house. She wondered if she should leave a note for Ed, give it to Piet at the airport. Or to Irma Stratton to give to him. She even thought of what she would put in it. There would be nothing in it to hint at how she felt. It would be a light-hearted farewell because that was how he would prefer it to be.

But she didn't get up to write it.

Next morning she could see the blue trimaran from the window of the jet-liner as the plane circled above the harbour before heading in an easterly direction towards the wide wastes of the Atlantic Ocean.

Jilly looked away and down at the magazine open on her knees and thought of all the things she hadn't done on the island. She hadn't been to visit Jules Martin in his pretty old French villa, painted pink and grey and overlooking Caracet Harbour. What was the old man thinking of his grandson's forthcoming marriage. Did he approve?

She hadn't been aboard Ed's boat, the fast three-hulled craft which he had sailed single-handed so successfully across oceans. He liked being by himself, he had once told her, enjoyed the days alone on the ocean, totally dependent on his own resources and his own abilities to cope with wind and weather. That should have warned her, shouldn't it? If he enjoyed his own company so much he didn't need a permanent relationship with a woman.

So how long would he stay married to Carol Stacey? The thought crept into her mind insidiously and she tried to banish it. But it would keep recurring. Nothing lasted for ever, she reminded herself sadly, not even marriage.

CHAPTER EIGHT

THE weather in England was much wetter and cooler than she had anticipated, and on the train journey to Portsmouth Jilly shivered in her jeans and cotton windbreaker. But the warm welcome that greeted her at the railway station when she emerged from the train made up for the grey skies and damp winds. Not only was her sister Valerie there to meet her but so were both her parents, having driven in from Felton to spend the day shopping.

'You look great, Jilly,' enthused Val. 'And what a wonderful tan. Doesn't she look wonderful, Mum?'

'Better than when you went away from here, at any rate,' said Ena Merrithew, kissing Jilly's cheek. 'The tropics seem to have agreed with you, but it was a good idea to come back before it got too hot out there.'

'Glad to have you back, Jilly. You're an answer to my prayers,' said Tom Merrithew. 'I'm behind on my orders, and now one of the machinists has hurt her hand and is off work. You've come back just when I need a sailmaker who knows what she's doing.'

The tourist and yachting season in the islands had been ending when she had left but in the south of England it had not long begun. Soon Jilly was feeling as if she had never been away as she became involved in her father's business once again. Every day she went with him to the sail-loft near the boatyard on the shores of Felton Creek, east of Portsmouth, in the same way she had driven every day to

Piet Block's boatyard on St Mark's, but instead of seeing the
green and gold waters of Town Bay every time she looked
out of a window, instead of palm trees, she saw mud-flats if
the tide was out, and the fresh green of beech trees coming
into leaf on the opposite shores of the creek. There were no
glimpses, either, of a tall wide-shouldered man with shiny
black hair to make her heart miss a beat.

All through May the boatyard sizzled with activity as
boats were launched and were sailed away to moorings in
front of Felton marina or to other marinas along the coast.
Soon Jilly was meeting again the many yachting people she
had known before she had left with the Turners. She found
that her absence had healed completely the wound made by
Kevin's death and that it was possible to go by the
apartment block in Portsmouth where they had lived
without any pangs of regret for what might have been if he
hadn't been killed. It was possible, also, to meet his relatives
and friends without feeling upset. She could remember him
with affection now and could smile when anyone
mentioned his name.

Someone had taken his place in her memories. Someone
who didn't deserve to be remembered or agonised over, she
told herself. Someone who was arrogant and selfish, for
whom she had been a pleasurable sideline while he had
been staying on St Mark's, only to be ignored and cast aside
when Carol Stacey had turned up. Someone whom she
intended to wipe from her memory as soon as she could find
the *Delete* key.

One day, towards the end of May, when she was in
Southsea, shopping for a dress for herself to wear at
Valerie's wedding, she ran into Simon Travis. In a neat
grey suit, white shirt and tie, his curly sun-bleached hair

trimmed in the latest masculine style, he looked very different from when she had last seen him, and she might have walked past him if he hadn't called out to her.

'Jilly! What are you doing here?' he exclaimed. They were near Southsea Common in one of the narrow shopping streets, and the wind that was blowing in off the sea held a hint of rain.

'I'm home for Val's wedding. She's getting married next week,' she explained. Only the deep ingrained tan of his face indicated that he had been at sea for weeks. 'When did you get back with Sue and Gerry?'

'Middle of April, some time.'

'Good crossing?'

'Slow but not bad even though that old tub rolls a lot.' He surveyed her curiously. 'How long are you going to be in Felton?' he asked.

'I'm not sure, I'm helping Dad out. He's behind on his orders as usual. I may stay all summer.' She grimaced at the rain which had begun to fall in earnest. 'That is if we're going to have one this year.'

'I know what you mean. When it's like this you yearn to be back in the islands, don't you?' Simon pushed back a cuff and glanced at his watch. 'I think I can safely say it's now lunchtime. How about having lunch with me now? Do you have time?'

'I'd like to.'

'Good. We can grab a ploughman's at the pub near the ferry terminus, in old Portsmouth, if you don't mind a quick walk,' he said and, opening his umbrella, held it over her head as they walked down the street to the common and turned right.

In the lounge of the pub which overlooked the busy old

harbour, Jilly made a great effort to be interested in Simon's account of his trip across the Atlantic with Sue and Gerry and, when he came to the end of anecdotes about that, she kept him talking by asking him how he was making out working for his father. Anything rather than have the position reversed and have him asking her questions about what she had done on St Mark's after he had left; anything rather than have him make some casual reference to Ed.

'Actually I'm rather enjoying working for the old man,' Simon admitted. 'Much more than I ever expected to. He's paying me well, too, which helps, even though I'm having to start right at the bottom and find out what it's like to be a grocer. I'm working in the store-rooms of his biggest store, here in Portsmouth, finding out all about the goods that are stocked, where they come from, why we stock them. Why some customers prefer one sort of tea to another. Which are the best canned goods to purchase. I'd no idea before that being a grocer required having a knowledge of geography as well as an eye for good quality and poor quality in the fresh goods. I'm also having to learn to use a computer. We use them all the time now for keeping inventories.' He glanced at his watch again. 'Time I wasn't here. Look, Jilly, can we meet again? Go to the cinema some night, or perhaps you'd prefer to go dancing?'

She arranged to meet him again and went home on the bus. When Valerie returned from her work as a quality-control supervisor in a local electronics company, they spent an hour on the last fitting of the wedding-dress of ivory silk and lace, and Jilly told her sister about meeting Simon again.

'That's good,' said Valerie, her pink-cheeked face serious

as she surveyed herself in a long mirror, turning this way and that to try to see whether the scalloped hem of the three-quarter-length dress was even. 'I mean it's good you have someone to go out with.' In the mirror she gave Jilly a curious glance from clear, round, hazel eyes set under dark, level brows. 'I thought when you came back that you looked great, but now you've been back a few weeks and some of your tan has faded I'm wondering if I was misled by that. You look as if you don't sleep very well. Coming back here hasn't made you start pining for Kevin again, has it?'

'No. In fact only the other day I was thinking how well I'd recovered from that. But you're right. I haven't been sleeping very well. It's taking me a while to become acclimatised, I suppose, after being in the tropics for so long.'

'Perhaps so,' murmured Valerie, but she didn't look convinced. 'You must have met a lot of interesting people out there. But the only ones you ever talk about are those two women, Marcha and Irma. Didn't you meet any interesting men?'

'Oh, yes. I've told you about Piet, and Raoul and Gerry.'

'But they were already attached. Wasn't there anyone unattached? Wasn't there anyone special, a man you liked more than any of the others?' Valerie's eyes twinkled with a sudden teasing laughter. 'I can't really believe you were out there all that time without having an affair with a handsome stranger, Jilly. I mean, think of the setting, palm-trees, sunshine, exotic blossoms, warm fragrances, the perfect romantic setting.'

Jilly knelt down on the floor, and tried to hide her face from her sister by examining the hem more closely.

'It isn't even, Val,' she said with a sigh. 'I'll have to

unpick this part and do it all again.'

'I knew it! I knew it!' Val exclaimed triumphantly. 'I guessed something romantic happened when you were on that island to give your eyes the far-away look they sometimes have. And now you've gone all pink.' She twitched the hem of her skirt from Jilly's fingers. 'The hem is perfectly all right. Nothing wrong with it. You just said that because you didn't want to answer my question. Hey, Mum! Guess what I've found out,' she said gaily as their mother came into the room. She began to dance about the room chanting, 'Jilly has a lover. Jilly has a lover. Or at least she had one in the tropics.'

'Val, if you don't shut up,' Jilly threatened, 'I won't finish your dress or come to your wedding.'

'You shouldn't talk like that about your sister,' Ena rebuked her younger daughter severely. 'I'm sure Jilly behaved herself as properly when she was away as she always has here. A lover, indeed! You watch too much telly, Val. One day you're going to wake up with a shock and find out that ordinary life isn't as it's portrayed in soap-operas.'

'Well, sometimes it is,' retorted the unrepentant Val. 'All right, all right, I won't tease you any more, Jilly,' she said with an endearing smile. Then as if to make amends she added lightly, 'You can ask Simon to the wedding if you like.'

'Thank you. I will,' replied Jilly primly, and she went out of the room rather than face her mother's suddenly curious eyes.

Simon was delighted to be invited to Val's wedding and duly escorted Jilly to the church, sat by her during the service and danced with her at the party afterwards.

Unfortunately while they were mingling with the other guests and sipping champagne he had to remind her of the evening in Caracet when he had suggested she return to England and marry him.

'I realised later that I chose the wrong moment, that you were irritated because of what people might think about you sharing that house with Ed Forster,' he explained. 'When you said you were having a torrid tropical affair with him I thought you were serious. I didn't realise you were being sarcastic. And I went and made a fool of myself at the marina. Did you stay on in that house?'

'No, I didn't. I moved out,' she said stiffly.

'That was wise. Well, anyway, all that's over and done with, and now we're both back on our home ground where we're both more likely to act normally, and I'd like you to know I'm still very keen on you, Jilly. The old man has been on to me about getting married and starting a family. Seems he would like one or two grandchildren. I wondered whether you would consider being engaged.'

'Engaged?' she repeated, giving him a puzzled glance.

'You know, the way our parents did things, the way Val and Rodney have done it. We announce that we're hoping to be married, I buy you a diamond ring and you wear it while we get used to the idea of getting married.'

'No,' she said abruptly. 'I don't mind going out with you occasionally, Simon, but I don't want to be engaged to marry you. Not yet. I . . . need more time . . .' Her voice trailed into silence.

'But I thought you'd got over Kevin's death,' he said. 'You seemed to have done so when we were on St Mark's,' he said with a touch of petulence. 'Look, Jilly, I know I'm a couple of years younger than you are but I'm really quite mature in my ways and I can offer you a lot. You wouldn't have to work once we were married and we could buy a decent sort of house, out in the country.'

'Simon, please stop,' she said laughing. 'You don't have to plead your cause like that. I know what you have to offer and I'm flattered, I really am, that you feel you would like to marry me. But I can't commit myself right now. I'm not ready. Now I hope you're not going to take offence and go off in a huff like the last time you asked me to marry you.'

'Not as long as you'll still go out with me. I'd like to take you to meet my father and my stepmother some time. He's bought the old manor house at Langlands and has renovated it. It's a beautiful place and of great historical interest. Would you like to visit it?'

'I'll think about it,' she murmured cautiously.

'We could go and stay for a weekend, leave here on Friday afternoon and come back Sunday evening.' Simon said enthusiastically as if she had already agreed to visit Langlands with him. 'I'll fix it up and let you know when.'

There were times during the next few weeks when Jilly felt she was three different personalities. She was Kevin's widow, young and still a little innocent in spite of having been married for a whole year to him and still hurting a little from the violence with which he had been wrenched away from her. She was also the sensual, passionate woman who had lived and worked on a tropical island and had indulged in a secret affair with a man notorious for his affairs with married women. And she was the rather coolly aloof unemotional woman who lived with her parents in the village of Felton, worked in her father's sail-loft and went about occasionally with Simon Travis, heir to that self-made millionaire, Henry Travis of the Easy-Save chain of groceries.

Valerie and Rod returned from their brief honeymoon in the Channel Islands and moved into the tiny town house they had bought in a suburb of Portsmouth. The weather for a while was good and Jilly went sailing several times with her father in his small day-boat.

Towards the end of the month there was a fierce storm which blew up suddenly and ravaged yachting in the English Channel and also in the Solent. Many racing boats capsized and some cruising yachts were dismasted. The storm was the talk of the yachting community in Felton all the following week. Suits of torn sails were brought to the sail-loft and Jilly and her father found themselves listening to many stories of near disaster, some of them told with dry humour. One story, which she heard on the morning of the Friday after the storm, caught Jilly's attention in particular. It was told by Rob Rowe who was a local boatbuilder and had been in the pub called the Compass Rose the night before with some of the yachtsmen who had been caught in the storm further down the coast near Plymouth, and had eventually put in there for safety.

'They were all in the bar of a pub down in the Barbican when in comes this American. They could tell he'd just come ashore because he was still in his foul-weather gear and was unshaven as if he'd been at sea for days. Someone asked him where he was from and he said he'd just arrived from Newport, Rhode Island in a race he'd had with an old friend to see who could break the record for the fastest crossing under sail single-handed. Someone recognised him as having been in Plymouth before and asked him how he fared in the storm. He raised his eyebrows and said, "What storm?"'

'Did he win the race?' asked Tom Merrithew.

'Nobody ever thought to ask him after that, apparently,' said Rob. 'But I do know he was sailing a trimaran and it's here now, anchored off the marina. It's blue and it's flying the French tricolour.'

'A lot of those big trimarans are designed and built in France,' commented Tom Merrithew, and the course of the conversation changed.

Itching to leave the loft and drive down to the marina to look out at the trimaran that was flying the French flag, Jilly stayed where she was at her machine stitching one of the damaged sails. It was just a coincidence that a trimaran registered as a French ship and sailed by a man who seemed to be an American was in Felton, she warned herself. The man referred to couldn't be Ed. Ed was in California, married to a woman called Carol, so how could he have been in Plymouth earlier that week and be in Felton now? And yet the story of the yachtsman who had just arrived from Newport and had raised his eyebrows and had said coolly 'What storm?' had the imprint of Ed's style on it.

She was still stitching the same seam when she heard her father calling to her, asking her to go down to the room below to look at something. She took her time, finishing the seam before descending the ladder into the big barn-like room below where sailcloth was stored. She looked round. Her father, lean and grey-haired, his hands on his hips, was watching another man who had longish untidy black hair and who needed a shave badly, pulling a sail out of a sailbag. At the foot of the ladder Jilly stood and stared, feeling the shock of surprise shiver through her. The man wasn't, he couldn't be Ed, she told herself. It was just someone who resembled him, and when he straightened up and looked at her she would know it wasn't him. No other man would have eyes as blue as his except his own father.

'I had it repaired in the Caribbean on St Mark's but I guess the sailmaker there didn't do a very good job. It split right down that same seam.' The drawling voice was so familiar that she closed her eyes tightly and clung with her hands to the ladder behind her.

'Looks to me as if the stuff is a bit thin there,' said Tom Merrithew, and turned to look across at Jilly. 'Come and look at this, Jilly. Think it will stand being repaired again?'

The man with the black hair looked up and right at her. She couldn't tell whether he was surprised to see her or not. His eyes were intensely blue.

'It would be easier to show you the split in it if the sail could be opened out,' he said. 'Perhaps up in the loft?'

'Good idea,' said Tom. 'This is my daughter, Jilly. She does a lot of the repairs we take in. Mr Forster has just come along the coast from Plymouth. He split his jib in that storm we had last weekend. He was near Land's End at the time. I'll be with you in about five minutes. I have to make a phone call.'

'But——' said Jilly, beginning to remonstrate with her father. He didn't seem to hear her and tramped away to his office in the corner of the big room. She looked back at Ed. He was staring at her with such a hostile expression in his eyes that she held on to the ladder even more tightly.

'Why did you leave the island without telling me?' he said in a rasping whisper.

'I don't think I have to answer that question. And I don't think you have any right to ask it,' she retorted. She stood there very straight knowing that she had gone pale. He shoved the part of the sail he had pulled out back into the sailbag, heaved the bag up on his shoulder and walked towards her. She didn't move. She couldn't. The sight of him seemed to have petrified her where she stood.

'Go on, up the ladder,' he ordered. 'Show me where the loft is like your dad said.'

'I ... I ...' she stammered and stopped, her tongue cleaving the roof of her mouth.

'I'm not surprised you have nothing to say,' he said, his lips curling in a jeering grin. 'Seeing me must have given you quite a shock. You never thought you'd have to explain why you left St Mark's without letting me know, without so much as a farewell note or maybe a kiss blown from your fingertips, did you?' he added through taut lips.

'Why should I have let you know?' she hissed, all the resentment she had felt towards him surging up suddenly and putting an end to her petrified state. 'You didn't explain anything to me. You didn't tell me you were going to be married to that big blonde woman and that was why you didn't want to have anything to do with me any more. So why should I take the trouble to tell you anything?'

It was as if the months since he had walked out that night in April had never been. It was if they were going to have the quarrel that they hadn't had then because he had left her in the middle of the night, refusing to quarrel.

The blue eyes blinked. The black eyebrows slanted in a frown.

'Now I'm fixed,' he drawled. 'I've no idea what you're talking about. I didn't tell you I was going to be married to some big blonde woman because I had no intention at that time of marrying anyone.' Someone stepped into the storage-room from outside and after a quick glance in the direction of the person, Ed leaned towards her. 'We can't discuss anything here. Get up that ladder. I'm sure you don't want your father or any of his clients hearing you argue with me. Go on.'

She turned at once and climbed the ladder. He was right as he so often was. She didn't want her father or any of his customers who might come in to hear them arguing with each other as only lovers argue.

In the loft he re-opened the sailbag and shook the sail out of it. Together they spread the triangle of dacron out. It was split in more than one place and was stiff with salt as if it had been soaked with sea-water. Kneeling, Jilly stared at it, imagining the beating it had taken before he had managed to haul it down.

'I heard about you,' she murmured. 'About how someone asked how you'd fared in the storm when you arrived in Plymouth and how you said "What storm?"' She clutched her cheeks between her hands as she imagined what it had been like out on the ocean, fighting the wind and the waves and the sails. 'Oh, you could have been swept overboard. You could have been drowned,' she whispered. 'Why do you do it? Why do you sail by yourself?'

'Because I've never found anyone I've wanted to sail with. And I couldn't have been swept overboard because I always wear a safety harness when I sail alone,' he replied coolly. 'See where it split, just where you stitched it?'

'But Dad is right. The material is worn. If I repair it again the sail will be smaller. I'll have to cut out the worn part. Or we could make you a new sail.'

'What's this? A sales pitch?' he jeered. 'Or are you trying to persuade me to hang around for a while so you can explain why you ran away from me?'

He had sat down on the floor beside her to examine the sail and when she turned to protest she found herself very close to him.

'I didn't run away from you,' she retorted and inched away from him along the floor. 'I came home to attend my sister's wedding.' She managed to get to her feet. 'There are other sailmakers in the area. You don't have to have your jib repaired here. And I wouldn't if I were you,' she went on with counterfeit sweetness, gaining confidence now that she wasn't so near him and he was still sitting while she was standing. 'Considering your opinion of the job I did on the sail in St Mark's.'

He grinned up at her and her heart leapt and her knees wobbled.

'I saw you come down the ladder, that's why I said that. And I've already been to all the other sailmakers in the area. They've all told me the same thing. Time I bought a new jib. I'd prefer to have this one repaired soon. I'm going over to France. I promised I would be there by Sunday,' he said, and rose to his feet in a lazy graceful movement. Stepping towards her he looked down at her with blazing blue eyes and said tautly, 'It's taken me a lot of foot-slogging today, lugging this sail about with me, to find you. And before that five weeks at sea, two from St Mark's to Newport and then eighteen days across the Atlantic, so I'm not about to fade out of your life just yet. I knew your father was a sail-maker near Felton, Piet had told me that, but I didn't know your family name before you were married.'

'Are you trying to tell me that you've come all that way just to see me?' she asked coolly. 'I don't believe you.'

'No. I'm not telling you that. I came across the ocean to

try and beat a friend of mine in a race, sailing single-handed. Since I happened to be in this country I thought I'd look you up.' His eyes sparkled with mockery and he leaned towards her. 'For old time's sake, sweetheart,' he whispered. 'I'm willing to bet you haven't forgotten yet what good times we used to have together on the island.'

His lips were only a hair's breadth from hers so she stepped back quickly, and behind one of the machines.

'Both Marcha and Irma know my address here. Why didn't you get it from one of them?' she countered.

'And risk having them guessing we'd had an affair after I'd gone to such pains to keep it a secret, to protect you from gossip?' he replied, stepping after her slowly, almost menacingly. Reaching out he seized hold of her shoulders and jerked her towards him. 'Couldn't you have waited one more day, one more night before flying back here?' he demanded.

'Why should I have waited?' She tried to shake her shoulders free of his grasp and failed, so she leaned back to get away from the temptation of his lips. 'Have you forgotten I was just as free as you were to come and go as I wished, when I wished, without informing you? A mistress isn't bound to a man in the same way as a wife is. But you know that. That's why you've never made any relationship with a woman permanent, isn't it?'

His face paled under the tan and bone showed white at the angle of his jaw. His fingers dug into her shoulders and she had to bite her lip to hold back a cry of pain.

'So, what's this?' he sneered. 'Convinced yourself at last, have you, that I was a brute who took all I could from you while I could and then got tired of you?'

'Yes, I have,' she retorted, her head held high as she

looked him in the eyes. 'And have you any idea how much you're hurting me now? Let go of me.'

Slowly his grasp on her shoulders slackened and his hand slid down her arms in a sort of caress that sent shivers through her. Dark lashes veiled his eyes and he caught a corner of his lower lip under the edge of his teeth. His breath came out in a long ragged sigh.

'I hate to admit it but I guess you're right. You were free to do as you wished,' he said in a low voice and, taking hold of her hands, he looked right into her eyes again, his own dark and stormy. 'But in self-defence I have to tell you, I went to the yard the day after the carnival with the intention of seeing you and you alone.'

'Why did you go to see me?' she managed to ask at last in a hoarse voice, unable to look away from him as he drew her gently towards him.

'To ask you to go to California with me the next day,' he murmured. 'So can you imagine how I felt when Marcha told me you'd left barely an hour before? I felt as if I'd been kicked where it hurts a man most. Another new experience for me.' His lips twisted wryly.

'You were going to ask me to go with you to California?' she gasped.

'Yes, to stay there with me while I finished the details of selling my business there. After that I planned to ask you . . .' He broke off and glanced at the top of the ladder that jutted up through the opening in the floor. 'Someone is coming up,' he murmured.

'Probably Dad.' she whispered but didn't pull away from him. He looked down at her, a swift smile lighting up his face. Her knees wobbled, her head whirled and she felt he sweet warmth of his lips against hers. Then the ladder rattled and he let her go. They both turned to look. Instead of Tom Merrithew, Simon Travis stood at the top of the ladder. He was staring at them.

'Jilly,' Simon began and paused, his eyes narrowing.

'You remember Simon, don't you, Ed?' she said brightly.

'Good to see you, Simon,' Ed wasn't in the least disconcerted and stepped towards Simon, his right hand out-stretched 'Tell me, is Jill any good as a sailmaker?'

'Oh, yes.' Simon's voice creaked a little as if he had forgotten how to use it. 'And her father is one of the best in this area. Makes racing-sails all the time.' He glanced down at Jilly. 'About the weekend,' he added more self-assertively, 'it's all fixed. I'll pick you up later, about six-thirty, from your place. Dad and Moira are expecting us for dinner and hope we'll stay until late Sunday. All right with you?'

'Fine with me,' she said smiling at him in a way she had never smiled at him before, and he responded in a way that she had never expected. Turning to Ed he said with a touch of defiance, 'Jilly and I are thinking of getting married soon.'

'That so?' drawled Ed at his most laconic. 'Seems to be the year for weddings. When I leave here I'll be going over to France to be at my sister's wedding, in Paris.' He glanced at Jilly. He seemed to be having difficulty in not laughing and she wondered what could have amused him. 'I was hoping you would come to her wedding with me, Jill. It says on the invitation I can take a partner. But since you and Simon are thinking of getting married,' he put a mocking emphasis on the word 'thinking', 'I guess you won't want to be my partner.' He shrugged and turned towards the ladder. 'I'll leave the jib with you, Jill. Hope you can get it repaired in time. See you both.'

Jill waited until she was sure he was out of earshot and then turned on Simon.

'Why did you say that, about us thinking about getting married?' she hissed.

'Well, why was he kissing you?' he retorted. 'And there's something about him that just gets my goat, the way he looks at you as if he knows something about you the rest of us don't,' he replied truculently. 'Anyway it won't do any harm for him to know you're not available to go to a wedding with him in Paris.'

'But don't you see what you've done?' groaned Jilly. 'He'll probably say something to my father about you and me thinking of getting married and then I'll have to face questions from Mother and from Val about when we're announcing our engagement. Oh, Simon, you are a dolt. And what makes you believe I wouldn't like to go to his sister's wedding? I would. I'd love to go to a wedding in Paris with Ed.'

The words were hardly out of her mouth than she realised what she had implied and she could tell by the way Simon scowled that he had taken offence. If only she hadn't tacked on the words 'with Ed'.

'I see, oh yes, I see very clearly now,' he said, tight-lipped. 'You've been expecting him to turn up here, haven't you? Hoping that he would come. You probably arranged to meet again here before you left St Mark's. That's why you've been so off-hand about going about with me. Yes, you're right, I am a dolt. A blind fool. But not any more. The invitation to come to Langlands at the weekend is off, definitely off. I'll take someone else. You're not the only woman in my life, Jilly Carter.'

He turned away and went down the ladder so fast she was sure he missed the last few rungs. It was hardly the easiest way to make a dignified exit after the dramatic declaration he had just made, thought Jilly, as she followed him. But she wasn't entirely amused. She was worried now in case he marched into the office and made some remark to her father about her having an affair with Ed as he had done at the marina bar on the island.

She reached the door to the office just behind him. In front of her he pulled up short and she bumped into him. Only her father was in the office, going through some files in his antiquated filing-system. He looked round in surprise, peering over his reading glasses at Simon.

'Hello there, Simon,' Tom Merrithew said mildly. 'Looking for Jilly? I think she's in the loft.'

'No, I'm not. I'm right here,' she said, stepping past Simon. 'Did Mr Forster tell you he wants me to repair his jib, Dad?'

'No. Haven't seen him since he went up to the loft with you.'

At that, with a muffled curse, Simon swung on his heels and left the office abruptly, banging the door behind him.

Tom glanced at Jilly with raised eyebrows.

'What's got into him?'

'He's angry about something I said to him,' said Jilly, and drew a deep breath. 'Dad, I think I ought to tell you that I knew Ed Forster when I was on St Mark's and that I repaired that jib he's just brought in.'

'Mmm, he didn't seem to be very pleased with what you'd done,' remarked Tom, flicking through files. 'Now where is the damned thing? I was sure I filed it under Mainsails,' he muttered.

'We, Ed and I, were very friendly,' Jilly continued, thinking how difficult it was to impart information about her personal life to her father. Perhaps she ought to tell her mother instead and let her pass the information on to Tom. Then she discarded the idea, guessing that her very moral mother, who was a strict traditionalist at heart, would not only be shocked if she learned that her elder daughter had indulged in a steamy love affair while she had been in the tropics, but she would also think that it was her fault in some way, that she had failed in her duty as a mother. No, it would be best if her mother never knew about what had happened between herself and Ed. Ena would only blame herself, and worry herself to death about it.

'Were you?' said Tom absently and, with an exclamation of triumph, he found and pulled out the file he had been searching for. 'Here it is. The design of the Turners' sails. I forgot to tell you. I had a letter from Reg Turner, from Annapolis in Maryland. He's going south to the islands in October, down the coastal waterway of the eastern States and then next spring he'll sail back here. He asked if you were still in St Mark's. He also sent an order for a new mainsail. Wants it delivered to that company you were working for. Says he'll pick it up there.'

With a sigh Jilly stepped in front of him as he made his way towards his design table.

'Dad, you didn't hear what I said, did you?'

'Yes, I did. You said something about having been friendly with Ed Forster when you were in St Mark's. So what am I supposed to say? You're a big girl now, Jilly. Have your own life to live. It isn't my place to pass judgement on any friendships you might have made while you were away in the islands. If he's a friend of yours why don't you ask him round to the house to meet your mother? I dare say he could do with some home cooking after being at sea by himself all those weeks.'

'How can I ask him home when he's gone off and left his jib behind and I don't know where he's gone?' argued Jilly. 'Oh, it's all Simon's fault. Why did he have to turn up when he did and say what he did?'

'No good asking me,' said Tom with a grin. 'What did he say?'

'He said that he and I were thinking of getting married,' Jilly seethed.

'I see. And aren't you?'

'No. Of course not. And now Ed's gone off believing that what Simon says was true and I'll never see him again, and never get the chance to go to Michelle's wedding.'

'I'm not really sure I know what all this is about,' said Tom, ruffling his tufts of grey hair. 'But one thing you can be pretty sure of, Forster will be back for his jib and he'll expect it to be repaired, so you'd better get started on it. There's still an hour and a half to go before we close up shop.'

CHAPTER NINE

JILLY was in her bedroom that evening getting ready for bed when the door opened and Valerie rushed in.

'Jilly, the most hilarious thing happened tonight down at the Compass Rose. I just had to come and tell you,' Val panted and flopped down on the bed. 'But first of all tell me if it's true you turned Simon down for a second time this afternoon?'

'I told him that I wasn't thinking of marrying him even if he was thinking of marrying me. You can call that turning him down if you like,' said Jilly cautiously.

'But it was for the second time, wasn't it?' Val persisted. 'He said you turned him down when you met him in St Mark's in February. Did you?'

'Yes, I did. But who told you?' Jilly turned back the sheets and blanket and slid into the bed.

'He did. Rod and I called in for a drink on our way home from town and Simon was in the bar. He saw us and came over to us. He was quite high. Slopped his drink all over the table when he put it down. And then he started on about you. "I'm talking about your sister, Val, your holier-than-thou elder sister," he kept repeating over and over again. "Twice now I've asked her to marry me and she's turned me down. Once in St Mark's and once this afternoon." And then he began to call you the most awful names, implying that your morals are loose and that you sleep around all the time. Rod told him to shut up and clear out, but he

166

wouldn't. We had just decided to leave so that he couldn't go on any more—everyone in the bar was listening to him—when this big man with the most gorgeous blue eyes came over, gave me the most charming smile and said, "Excuse me, folks, but I've had just as much as I can take from this snivelling little shrimp,"—only he didn't call Simon just a shrimp. I can't repeat the adjective he used. Anyway, "It's time he went home to his mother," he added, and then he got hold of Simon's shirt collar, heaved him up out of the chair and dragged him out of the pub.'

'Oh, no,' Jilly groaned and buried his face on her hunched knees.

'Oh yes,' Val gabbled on. 'Rod and I couldn't believe it for a few moments and neither could anyone else. Then we rushed for the door. We all wanted to see what Blue Eyes would do to Simon, you see. I suppose we were all hoping he would punch him up.'

'But he didn't, did he?' asked Jilly in a horrified whisper.

'No.' Val actually sounded disappointed. 'He just lugged Simon over to his car and pushed him into the back seat. And then, I suppose, he must have got the keys out of Simon's pocket. Anyway he got in the driver's seat and drove it away. He sounded as if he was an American and last seen he was driving on the wrong side of the road. But he must have realised his mistake because we didn't hear him collide with anything coming the other way and so far I haven't heard of any traffic accidents.'

'But where would he take Simon?' asked Jilly, raising her face from her knees.

'To his home, I suppose. He seemed to know Simon. Who was he—Blue Eyes, I mean? Do you know him? He was dressed in sailing togs, wore a yellow waterproof jacket

over jeans and a navy-blue jersey. His hair was black and
I've told you about his eyes.' Val's own eyes danced with
curiosity.

'Yes, I know him. He's Ed Forster. I met him in St
Mark's. So did Simon.' Jilly groaned again and clutched
her head. 'Now, what am I going to do? It'll be all over the
village tomorrow. How could Ed make a scene like that?'

'If you ask me it was Simon who started it all, getting
drunk and then foul-mouthing you. Ed stopped him, thank
goodness.' Val leaned forward, her eyes shining now with
admiration. 'I thought he was great. And you must feel
really honoured to have someone like him to come to your
defence. It's like one of those tales of romantic chivalry,
with the knight errant rescuing the fair maiden, only
you're a fair widow, not a maiden.'

'Val, you haven't said anything to Mum and Dad about
this?' asked Jilly urgently.

'No. Mum had gone to bed when we got here. But I
expect Rod will have told Dad by now. I left them in the
kitchen together. But why don't you want Mum to know?'

'Because she'll get all worked up about it, and start on
one of the those guilt-trips she goes in for sometimes,
thinking the worst as usual, and that she's to blame for the
way you or I behave. She'll start saying it's all because she
went out to work when we were growing up instead of
staying with us all the time.'

'Mmm. I know what you mean,' sighed Val. 'You'd think
she'd never been in love herself or ever had passionate
urges, wouldn't you?' Val laughed suddenly. 'Maybe that's
why she worries about us. Maybe she was passionate when
she was younger and had an affair with someone who didn't
want to marry her. Maybe that's why she's so prim and

proper now. Anyway if Rod has told Dad she's bound to hear all about it. He tells her everything.'

Jilly couldn't decide the next morning whether her parents knew anything about the incident at the Compass Rose because neither of them said anything about it to her and she didn't mention it to them. She really should move into a place of her own, she thought, as she drove to the sail-loft in her father's small van. Her parents had reached a time in their lives when they didn't want a grown daughter living with them. The problem was the same as the one she had had in St Mark's. Where could she find a flat or rooms she could afford on the pay she earned working for her father?

Alone at the sail-loft because the other sailmakers didn't work on a Saturday and her father had gone somewhere with her mother for the day, she continued with the repair to Ed's jib, hoping that he would call in to collect it that afternoon.

By four o'clock she had finished repairing the sail. She folded it and stowed it in the bag. By five o'clock Ed hadn't come for it so she decided to take it down to the marina and leave it with the manager there to give it to Ed when he saw him.

It was a lovely afternoon, the sun warm and a light breeze blowing from the south-west. A few boats were lolling about on the Solent, their sails shimmering. Arriving at the marina she parked the van and carried the sailbag into the office. Lugging the sailbag after her she walked to the marina office. Only a young man who kept an eye on the boats was there.

'I'm looking for Ed Forster,' she said. 'I have a sail here for him. Is his boat still here?'

'It's out there.' He pointed to the few boats which were at anchor or on moorings. She recognised the blue hulls and glinting gold masts immediately. 'He hasn't been ashore today. Like me to take the sail out to him for you?'

'I think it would be best if I delivered it personally to him. There are a few explanations to be made,' she said, coming to a sudden and rather surprising decision. 'Could you take me out to his boat in the launch?'

'Sure.'

Within a few minutes she was sitting in the bow of the sturdy varnished motor-boat as it powered over the water in the direction of the trimaran. As he approached the multi-hulled craft the young man slowed the launch down and guided it carefully between the slim port hull or *ama*, as the two outer balancing hulls of a trimaran are called, and the centre hull. Jilly managed to heave the sailbag aboard and then get up and into the cockpit. The launch reversed away from the centre hull and, turning, headed back to the marina.

For a while Jilly sat in the cockpit listening to the noise of the launch's engine fade. The blue boat rocked gently on the waves churned up by the motor-boat and fittings on the two aluminium masts clinked. Stainless-steel rigging and winches glinted in the pale sunshine. The trimaran looked clean and shipshape but its exterior woodwork was in need of varnish, hinting that it had spent weeks at sea. Designed for speed, the centre hull was long and narrow, and housed the cabin. The main hatchway was open and behind the hull, tied on by its painter, was a small rubber dinghy, easy to bring up on deck and deflate, to stow aboard. The fact that the dinghy was there meant that Ed was on the boat somewhere. She waited another fifteen minutes, enjoying the pleasant scene and the quiet peace of being away from the land, then leaned forward and called into the cabin.

'Ed. Are you down there? I've brought your jib. It's repaired.'

He didn't appear in the hatchway and he didn't answer her so she went forward and stepped down a short ladder into the narrow cabin. Near the hatchway on the port side there was a galley fitted with a sink and stove. On the starboard side opposite was a wide chart-table. Above it on a shelf was a radar screen, a VHF radio and other electronic navigational equipment. Further forward in the centre of the cabin there was only one berth, a fairly wide one. On it Ed was lying, apparently fast asleep.

Accustomed as she was to the comparatively luxurious cabins of Reg Turner's ketch, Jilly stared in amazement at the emptiness of the cabin, wondering how Ed had lived for days and weeks in such conditions. Slowly she sat down on the side of the double bunk and then let her glance slant down at him. Only once before had she seen him asleep. That first time, the morning she had been awakened by Irma phoning her, and then she hadn't paused to study him while he slept.

Now she could feast her eyes on him, she thought. After nearly three months of separation from him she could indulge herself, gloating on the shininess and silkiness of his black hair, the leanness of his sun-tanned face, the bold Norman nose, the thick black eyelashes, the sensual curve of his wide lips. He was wearing only a white singlet which showed off the bulges of shoulder and bicep muscles beneath skin tanned to a teak colour by the sun. A froth of dark hair showed just above the low curving neck-line of the singlet. The rest of him was hidden by a quilted sleeping-bag.

As she looked at him she felt the now-familiar knot of desire begin to tighten up within her. It was accompanied by an upsurge of emotion, a torrent of feeling that she had kept damned back ever since she had left St Marks.

'Oh, Ed,' she whispered, sliding on to her knees beside the bunk. 'I'm so glad you came here to have your jib repaired.'

Tentatively she touched his face with her fingers, then giving into her tumultuous feelings she laid her cheek against his. The familiar fragrance of him wreathed itself about her and turning her lips to his she kissed them.

To her surprise his lips responded, pressing against hers. She tried to withdraw and found herself trapped by his arm about her shoulders, holding her down.

'I was thinking I would have to leave without seeing you again,' he whispered.

'Without your jib?' she queried.

'I have another, the one you really repaired in St Mark's,' he said, his lips slanting with wicked humour. 'The one you've just repaired is an old one. I used it as an excuse to look for you.'

'Then you didn't need it in a hurry after all and I needn't have spent most of today repairing it,' she complained. 'You devil!' She would have pulled away from him and stood up but his arm bound her close to him. Forcing her lips down to his he kissed her again and for a while there was silence as they kissed urgently, lips parted and tongues probing avidly.

Somehow he managed to lift her on to the bunk until they were lying close together. Somehow the sleeping-bag was unzipped and spread over both of them. They kissed hungrily, tenderly, bruisingly, achingly. They didn't speak. They didn't have to. Their hands and lips were doing their communicating for them as all their pent-up passion for each other burst forth, overwhelming all inhibitions and blotting out the pain of separation.

'It's good to be close to you, to hold you, to feel you, to smell you,' murmured Ed as he stroked the blouse she was wearing from her shoulders and breasts. 'God only knows how much I've missed your softness and warmth. Not until I realised you'd left the island had I ever felt lonely before, especially in the night.'

It was unbelievable. He was actually admitting to having missed her!

'I couldn't stay when I heard from Marcha and then from Irma that you were going to marry that blonde woman, Carol Stacey. I couldn't stay knowing you were on the island but you weren't coming to see me any more,' Jilly murmured, her breasts lifting and hardening to the gentle drift of his fingers. 'I knew you didn't love me as I loved you. I thought it was all over between us. I thought that was why you walked out that night.' She pressed herself close to him, hiding her face against his chest as tears welled in her eyes at the remembered anguish of those days at the end of April when he hadn't come to visit her. He stroked her hair soothingly then her nape with gentle seduction. She sighed with pleasure, turning her lips to his throat, licking the hollow at its base.

'I walked out that night because I wasn't ready to make a commitment to you. I had problems to solve before I could do that but I didn't want to quarrel with you because I knew I'd want to come back to you,' he whispered into her hair.

'After you had married Carol?' she asked suspiciously. 'You dared to think I would continue to be your mistress, the woman you could visit every time you came to St Mark's?'

'I told you yesterday I had no intention of marrying Carol,' he retorted. 'That idea was dreamed up by Michelle when she came back from France up to her ears in debt and found the Staceys staying with me. While I was in California I'd interested Clark Stacey in buying my business there. I invited him and Carol over to the island so that we could continue bargaining. Michelle thought it would be a great idea if we sold Clark the House of Doves too. I objected to selling it so she came up with the totally ridiculous suggestion of me marrying Carol to keep the house in the family. She didn't tell me she was broadcasting her idea to the island, to Irma and Martha,' he growled. 'Just wait until I see her,' he added threateningly. Winding his fingers in her hair he jerked her head back so that he could see her face. 'And how dare you believe rumours about me?' he added with silky menace. 'You could easily have asked me whether the rumour was true.'

'How could I when you went to such lengths to avoid me?' she challenged him. 'How could I when you had made it clear you didn't like me to ask you questions about yourself? How could I without breaking the guidelines? You were just as much to blame for my leaving the island as any rumour I heard.'

'Shut up,' he ordered, and silenced her with a kiss that went on for a long time. Slowly and suggestively his hand slid up her thigh and, as the gentle caress of his fingers drew from her the familiar rhythmic response, she abandoned further argument and gave herself up to the pleasure of rousing him, revelling in the sensations she experienced by caressing his skin and feeling the excited throb of his passion-fired blood, hearing his unrestrained groans and gasps and, at last, feeling the hard thrust of his desire as he plunged into the dark mysterious depths of her own desire. For a few moments they were one, moving in unison, crying out together, then laughing together as the fulfilling climax of passion was reached, then sighing as it subsided, leaving them lying entwined in a cocoon of warmth beneath the sleeping-bag.

It was then, in those tranquil moments of aftermath, that Jilly dared to say how she felt,

'I love you,' she whispered, and held her breath.

He didn't move. His head stayed where it was, heavy against her breast, and after a while he said with just the suspicion of laughter drawling his voice, 'I thought I'd warned you never to say that to me.'

'You did, but I have to say it because it's true,' she said, tangling her fingers in his hair.

'And what would you like me to say?' he growled.

'That I'm the only woman in the world for you, might be a start,' she teased, then added more urgently, 'No, just tell me what you feel, truly feel, about me.'

'Haven't I just shown you how I feel? Didn't I sail all those miles to find you? What more do I have to do to prove that I . . .' he broke off tantalisingly.

'That you what? Oh, you can't stop in the middle of a sentence like that,' she complained, pulling his hair.

'Ouch.' He raised his head, smiled at her and her bones seemed to melt. 'I guess I must be in love with you,' he drawled. 'I began to suspect I was when I was in California,' he went on, shifting onto his back and pulling her against him until her head rested on his shoulder. 'I found I didn't want to be there. I wanted to be back on the island with you. And it occurred to me then that all I had ever wanted was there, on the island where I'd been born. So I decided to sell the busines in California and then invest what I made from the sale in Piet and Marcha's business, become their partner in the fullest sense.' He sighed heavily and with exasperation. 'I had it all worked out, but I didn't take into account any problems you and Michelle might create.'

'You could have told me what you wanted to do when you came back from California, then I wouldn't have created a problem,' she pointed out.

'I guess I could have, but I wasn't ready. There was still a possibility I wouldn't be able to pull off the deal with Stacey. He's a tough customer when it comes to bargaining. I had to keep at him all the time. That's one reason why I didn't come to see you. I didn't want to come to you again until I had everything straight. Not until I had cleared myself of that mess could I come to you again. I got rid of the Staceys, persuaded Michelle to return to France and felt I was free at last to go to you. But you'd left the island.' He paused, then went on in a low voice, 'For the first time I really understood how Pierre felt when he found Paulette had eloped with me. And you weren't my wife.'

There was a short tense silence. Again Jilly was having difficulty in believing that she was lying in his arms and he was confiding in her.

'I wish I'd known,' she moaned. 'I wouldn't have left if I'd known. But I couldn't bear knowing you were on the island and not being with you. Remember once you said to me what hell it was living in the same house and not having each other? Well, that was what it was like for me after you walked out that night.'

'I remember. I remember everything we said and did vividly. I'd never known anyone like you before and every moment with you was a shared delight imprinted for ever on my memory. But it wasn't until Marcha told me you were on that plane that it struck me why I felt like that about you. Then I realised I loved you more than anyone else I'd ever known.'

'More than you'd ever loved Paulette?' she had to ask. She had to know to exorcise the devil of jealousy which still rode her when she thought of his life before she had met him.

'I never loved Paulette. I only imagined I did. I was infatuated with her.' His voice grated in self-derision.

'She must have been very beautiful,' she murmured, not because she believed Paulette had been beautiful but because she had felt him stiffen and guessed he would have preferred not to talk about his elopement experience.

'She was,' he growled. 'And flighty.'

'Was that why you didn't stay with her?' she persisted.

'No.' He was very abrupt, then just when she was thinking he wasn't going to say any more he added drily, 'She ditched me. I didn't ditch her. It was her idea that we should elope, not mine. And I guess I was flattered because she seemed to prefer me to Pierre. I couldn't see that she was using me.' He laughed shortly. 'I thought she was in love with me, was crazy about me and that we were going to have a wonderful sexy affair together. In reality I was merely her chauffeur, driving her to meet another man, her real lover.'

'You mean she pretended to elope with you to hide the fact that she was going off with another man?' gasped Jilly.

'You've got it, first time,' he said bitterly. 'When we got to Nice she required nothing more of me and went off with him.'

'How did you feel?' she whispered, empathising with the young and vulnerable person he had been then. 'When you found out she had used you?'

'Mad and hurt. But mostly mad as hell because she'd been able to take me for a ride. I went back to tell Pierre what had happened only to find he'd shot himself and that my name was muck in my mother's family because I had led Paulette astray and not the other way round. Nobody would listen to what I had to say, except my grandfather. He was the only one who had guessed what Paulette was like, possibly because he had had a similar experience with a woman. I guess it was after that I decided I might as well live up to the reputation I'd earned, without really trying, as a stealer of other men's wives.' Once more his voice rasped with remembered bitterness.

'I guessed it was a fiction, a pretence,' she whispered, trailing her lips along the clean-cut edge of his jaw. At last they were really close, she thought in a haze of happiness. At last he was sharing his secrets, his past with her.

'It wasn't entirely a pretence,' he drawled warningly. 'Don't ever make the mistake of believing that it was, but until I met you I'd never had an affair with an innocent, unattached woman like you. I was attracted to you from our first meeting when you would have slit my throat if I'd made a wrong move, but afterwards I was scared stiff your good name might be damaged if it got around the island that you were associated in any way with me. It was a new experience, wanting you yet having to protect you from myself at the same time. Made me see what I'd become over the years, selfish and cynical.' He drew a deep breath. 'In a way I wasn't surprised you left St Mark's when you did. I decided you'd had enough and had realised that I wasn't worthy of your love. I flew back to California to arrange the take-over of the business there by Clark Stacey, and went back to the island to buy Michelle's share of the house. I'd done what I'd wanted to do. There was just one thing missing. You, the reason why I'd sold the business and become sole owner of the House of Doves.'

'Were you mad?' she asked.

'For a while I was. I hated you for having been able to get under my skin. I sat in that house on the cliffs and brooded, haunted by you flitting about the terrace in your nightie,' he said, bitterly self-mocking. 'When I couldn't stand it any more I put to sea and ended up in Newport. I ran into an old friend there and he challenged me to a race across the ocean to Plymouth. He said he would beat me. I could never refuse a dare. And here I am,' he said.

'You wouldn't have come if you hadn't received the challenge, then,' she asked. The ache of tears that she had known when she had asked him questions the last time was back in her throat. Tensely she waited for his reply.

'I know you would like me to say I would have come looking for you,' he murmured, turning her face up to his. 'But that wouldn't be true, and I've always tried to be honest with you. I wouldn't have followed you deliberately, because I felt you would really be better off without someone like me in your life. Marcha did say you would be back on the island in the October. I had intended to wait until you returned and take it from there.' He shifted her on to her back so that he could lean over her. Dark and tormenting, his glance roved over her face, her throat, her

breasts. 'But why waste precious time talking about what
didn't happen, and won't happen now. We've met again,
we're together again and I'm feeling this great urge to kiss
you again. You're so sweet, Jilly, sweet and soft, and I've
been through hell the past few months wanting you and not
having you.'

There was no way she could resist such an appeal. Arms
about him she held him closely.

'Me too,' she sighed, her eyes closing as she sank down
under the hot tide of his passion.

Some time later she became aware of the sound of
rushing water and opened her eyes. She was lying alone on
the bunk, naked beneath the quilted sleeping-bag. The
slant of light through the narrow ports informed her that it
was late evening. Her glance went to the brass nautical
clock on the bulkhead and she verified the time on her
watch. Five minutes past nine. Her parents must be
wondering where she was.

She sat up quickly. There was no doubt that the trimaran
was moving. Hastily she pulled on her clothes, stepped into
her deck-shoes and climbed up the ladder into the cockpit.
The cool wind whipped against her, moulding her blouse
against her breasts. Her hair lifted and fanned out like a
halo around her head.

Ed was sitting on one of the narrow cockpit seats holding
the tiller. Wearing an orange survival-suit he was looking
up at the sails which were bellying with wind, pulling the
boat forward. Behind him the land was a low dark line
starred with the twinkle of lights from streets and houses.
They were so far away from it Jilly couldn't make out the
shape of buildings or see the masts of other boats in the
marina. Looking forward she saw another dark mass of

land, starred with lights, the Isle of Wight. The boat was out in the middle of the Solent where the lights of navigational buoys blinked red and green.

'What are you doing?' she exclaimed.

'Trying out the jib you so kindly repaired and brought to me,' Ed replied, his grin flashing in his darkened face.

'But it's after nine. We must go back. Mother and Dad will be wondering where I am.'

'We're not going back. At least not now. We're going to France, we should be there, if this wind keeps up, by tomorrow morning. And you don't have to worry about your people. I radioed the marina before I set sail and asked Chris Hampton to give them a message.'

'What did you tell him to tell them?' she demanded, hugging her arms about her. In a summer skirt and blouse she wasn't dressed for night-sailing and she was still amazed that they were so far away from land. She must have slept very deeply because she hadn't heard him moving about and preparing to leave the anchorage.

'I said you'd eloped. With me,' he drawled.

'You didn't!' she gasped in consternation.

'Not in as many words. I just said you'd gone with me to my sister's wedding and that you'd be back next week. Maybe.' His grin was tantalising now.

'But I can't go to a wedding dressed like this.'

'So I'll buy you something glamorous in Paris. I'm not a bad hand at choosing women's clothes.'

'No doubt you have had plenty of experience,' she retorted. 'Seriously, Edouard Forster, I would like you to turn back and put me ashore.'

'Seriously, Gillian Carter,' he mocked 'I'm not turning back. I promised I would be in Paris by tomorrow evening and would attend the wedding on Monday.'

'You could have gone by ferry. Or even flown there,' she pointed out.

'I prefer to go this way and I want you to be with me. I'm not letting you out of my sight ever again. So shut up, and go down below to make us something to eat and drink. You'll find sweaters and boots and windbreakers in the locker up forward. I wouldn't want you to die of pneumonia while we're eloping.'

'You are the most stubborn, conceited man I have ever known,' she said grandly and, sticking out her tongue at him, she went hurriedly below.

It took her a while to find clothes and to struggle into them. It wasn't that the trimaran heeled more than a more traditional craft would have done. The two narrow outer hulls kept the central hull on an even keel so that the whole boat travelled much faster than it would have done if it had heeled. But there was a certain lurching movement which made balancing a little difficult, and then she had to spend time turning up sleeves and adjusting Ed's clothes to her own slighter figure.

Burrowing in a locker beneath the chart table, she found, as she had hoped, cans of soup, and soon she had one warming in a pan on the gimballed stove. And all the time she felt her heart was singing because she was there at last on Ed's boat and she was actually preparing a meal for him, something he had never let her do before. She was with him and they were eloping to France, like couples had done often in the past from England, eloping to get married . . .

Her thoughts skidded to a stop. How foolishly romantic could she get? He hadn't asked her to marry him. He probably never would.

When the soup was hot she poured it into two big mugs and then carried one of them up to the cockpit and handed it to Ed. The sky was fully dark apart from the usual light streaks in the north-west, and the stars were coming out. Never had she been at sea in that part of the world on such a beautiful night. Normally it was either blowing a gale or there was no wind at all.

'I don't know what my mother is going to think when she hears I've gone off in a yacht with a strange man,' she said, when with her own mug of soup in her hand she sat close to him in the cockpit.

'She doesn't know about us, then? You've never told her about me?' he asked.

'No. I haven't told any of them about you. Oh, Val, my sister, guessed that there'd been someone. And then yesterday I tried to tell Dad about you but he didn't want to hear. He said my life was my own to do what I liked with and my friendships had nothing to do with him. But Mother is different. She's very strict about morals. She doesn't care for permissiveness at all. I would think she has heard about you by now. Everyone in the village will know what happened in the Compass Rose last night and how you took exception to what Simon was saying about me. What did you do to Simon?'

He didn't answer for a few moments then he said with a ripple of amusement in his voice,

'I guess your sister told you all about it. Personally I'm glad Simon forgot himself and started calling you names. If he hadn't I'd have had a rough night of it trying to get over the fact that you and he were thinking of getting married.' He laughed. 'It was a bit like the time in St Mark's when he drank too much and started telling everyone we were having an affair. And he was more or less saying the same thing except his language was a bit more foul. I drove him to the place where he lives, sobered him up and gave him a good talking to, like an older brother might.' He paused and then added in a quieter voice, 'I also made it clear to him that, since I had every intention of making you my wife, I was glad he'd stopped thinking of marrying you himself.'

She sat still. The paean of joy and thanksgiving that had been singing through her mind was even louder, so loud she was sure he could hear it. Eventually she said teasingly, 'How can you make me your wife when you haven't asked me to marry you?'

'I'm eloping with you, aren't I? You'll have to marry me now to keep your good name,' he taunted.

'Is that the only reason you'd want to marry me?' she challenged. 'To protect my good name?'

'You know damned well it isn't,' he said softly, moving until he was beside her and could put his arm around her shoulders. Fingers under her chin he tilted it and kissed her on the mouth. 'I want to marry you so that I have the right to kiss you, to make love to you. So shall we do it, in Paris, after Michelle's wedding is over?'

'No,' she said coolly.

'Why not?' He had stiffened as he sensed rejection and his arm fell away from her.

'I want to be married properly, the way I was to Kevin, the way my parents were and my sister was. I want to do it openly, not covertly as if it's something to be ashamed of.' She turned to him, 'If you love me, really love me, you'll wait until we get back to Felton and inform my parents first. I'd like to be married to you in front of them, not behind their backs. If you can't agree, I won't marry you at all.'

The waves rushed against the hulls. The masts and booms creaked with the weight of wind in the sails. To Jilly's relief Ed's arm curved about her again, his bristly cheek rubbed against hers.

'I'm glad you don't want to do it covertly,' he whispered. 'I can wait to do it properly if you can. I've had enough of secrecy, too. If you knew the number of times I've wanted to shout my love for you from the roof tops.'

'Really?' she whispered in surprise.

'Really,' he mocked. 'And now if you don't mind I'd like to attend to sailing this boat. We're making good progress in this wind, about fifteen knots.'

'I didn't know a sailing-boat could go so fast,' she remarked.

'This one can go even faster in a gale of wind. That's why some of us prefer trimarans for racing across oceans,' he replied. 'Will you come with me when I sail it back to St Mark's? We could leave after we've been married. The trip could be our honeymoon.'

'I thought you preferred to sail alone,' she taunted.

'That was before I met you,' he retorted. 'Will you come with me?'

'I'll come,' she agreed wholeheartedly. 'I'm not going to be left behind when you go sailing. Not ever. You're single-handed days are over. You see, I'm not going to let you out of my sight ever again. I'm very possessive.'

'I had noticed,' he said with an amused chuckle, and he kissed her briefly but possessively. 'That makes two of us,' he added. 'But right now you're going to get out of my sight by going down below to sleep. I'll wake you in about two hours to go on watch while I have a rest, although I slept pretty well this afternoon, thinking I'd be making the crossing alone. I'm glad you brought that jib to me.'

'I'm glad I did too.'

'And thanks for repairing it. How much do I owe you?'

'It was a labour of love,' she replied gaily, and went down to the cabin.

By early morning they were off the French coast and saw the sun come up over Normandy. By noon they were anchored in the port of Le Havre where, Ed told her, his grandfather had been born and where he himself had become involved with Paulette. By evening they were in Paris and next morning, true to his word, he took her shopping for a dress to wear at Michelle's wedding.

Michelle, dark-eyed and vivacious, excited by her own marriage to a handsome man called Louis Verdun, was honestly surprised when she saw Jilly with her brother, but had no chance to comment until the ceremony was over. It was a very public wedding. Louis was a French screen idol and the reporters were out in force. Numerous photographs were taken, including one of Jilly and Ed with the happy couple. When Jilly saw it the day after in a Paris newspaper she carefully translated the caption to herself. Her name did not appear. She was just reported as being Monsieur Edouard Forster's bride-to-be.

'I'm very pleased to hear about you and Ed,' Michelle had said to her when leaving the reception the previous day for a honeymoon on the Riviera. 'He looks so relaxed, happier than I've ever seen him. Do you have any recipe I should know for making a man like that?'

'Not really,' Jilly had replied. 'Just a lot of loving. Never give up loving.'

As for Ena Merrithew, when informed that Jilly was going to marry Ed, after giving Ed a very close assessing stare, she merely remarked, 'I'm glad you have had the decency to ask her to marry you after the scene you made in the Compass Rose and after taking her with you on your boat to France. We wouldn't want her good reputation smirched.'

Watching Ed's face Jilly held her breath. To her relief his blue eyes smiled and he inclined his dark head politely to her mother.

'That's something about which you and I will always agree, ma'am,' he said softly, then turning to Jilly he winked at her outrageously.

'It's because she loves me that she said that,' Jilly explained in a whisper, defending her mother.

'And it's for the same reason that I agree with her, because I love you,' he said softly.

Bending his head he kissed her in full view of all her family, much to the delight of Valerie who applauded, clapping her hands together loudly, and Jilly's heart sang because their affair, that had begun secretly under tropical stars, had at last become public in the sunlight of a summer's day in England. No longer need they hide their love for each other. It was there, in the open, a joyful, generous emotion for all to see and admire.

*Exciting, adventurous, sensual stories
of love long ago*

On Sale Now:

SATAN'S ANGEL by Kristin James

*Slater was the law in a land that was as wild and untamed
as he was himself, but all that changed when he met
Victoria Stafford. She had been raised to be a lady, but
that didn't mean she had no will of her own. Their search
for her kidnapped cousin brought them together, but they
were too much alike for the course of true love to run
smooth.*

PRIVATE TREATY by Kathleen Eagle

*When Jacob Black Hawk rescued schoolteacher
Carolina Hammond from a furious thunderstorm, he
swept her off her feet in every sense of the word, and she
knew that he was the only man who would ever make her
feel that way. But society had put barriers between them
that only the most powerful and overwhelming love could
overcome . . .*

Look for them wherever Harlequin books are sold.

Lynda Ward's

... the continuing saga of *The Welles Family*

You've already met Elaine Welles, the oldest daughter of
powerful tycoon Burton Welles, in Superromance #317, *Race
the Sun*. You cheered her on as she threw off the shackles of her
heritage and won the love of her life, Ruy de Areias.

Now it's her sister's turn. Jennie Welles is the drop-dead-
gorgeous, most rebellious Welles sister, and she's determined to
live life her way—and flaunt it in her father's face.

When she meets Griffin Stark, however, she learns there's more
to life than glamour and independence. She learns about
kindness, compassion and sharing. One nagging question
remains: is she good enough for a man like Griffin? Her father
certainly doesn't think so....

Leap the Moon ... a Harlequin Superromance coming to you
in August. Don't miss it!